Millet, Lydia
The shimmers in t

F   MIL

# THE
# SHIMMERS
# IN
# THE
# NIGHT

# THE SHIMMERS IN THE NIGHT

*a novel*

## LYDIA MILLET

**Big Mouth House**
Easthampton, MA

Big Mouth House
150 Pleasant Street #306
Easthampton, MA 01027
bigmouthhouse.net
weightlessbooks.com
info@bigmouthhouse.net

Distributed to the trade by Consortium.

First Edition
September 2012

Library of Congress Control Number on file.

ISBN: 978-1-931520-78-2 (trade cloth); 978-1-931520-79-9 (ebook)

Text set in Minion Pro.
Printed on 50# Natures Natural 30% PCR Recycled Paper by C-M Books in Ann Arbor, MI.

*For Mrs. Merry and Mrs. B.*

*One*

*It was a Sunday in late October, the week before Halloween.*
Long drifts of red and yellow leaves covered the front yard of
the Sykes's rambling house next to Cape Cod Bay. A couple of
days ago it had been crisp outside, an average fall day—just
chilly enough so you could breathe in the cold air and notice
it had its own clean taste—but today it was warm. Cara wore
nothing but a cotton shirt, and even so she was sweating as
she raked. This must be what her dad called Indian summer.

But still, it was strangely warm.

She tramped through the piles of leaves around to the
side of the house, where a rusty thermometer stuck out of
the gray wooden shingles. The red line of mercury hovered
at seventy-four.

It was Jax's job to rake and bag the leaves; he got paid a
big five bucks, which their dad seemed to think was a wind-
fall. "When *I* was ten years old," he said sternly, "I mowed
the lawn for a nickel. And I was happy to do it." But Jax
was in Cambridge for two weeks at some kind of genius-kid
camp run by an institute her older brother, Max, called "a
think tank."

Max said he wouldn't trust those think-tank people as
far as he could throw them. He said "think tank" basically

1

meant *place full of evil smart people*, because a place full of *harmless* smart people was called "a university."

Max (being a rebel, or at least liking to look like one) thought there were conspiracies all around them. The night before Jax left, Max had spun out a few paranoid scenarios for their baby brother's benefit as the three of them sat in Max's chaotic bedroom, littered with dirty vintage T-shirts, Ramones and Clash posters pinned messily to the walls. It was entirely possible, he'd told Jax, that the people who worked at the think tank only *pretended* they were going to teach him how to "optimize the skills associated with his eidetic memory" as they'd said in their letter. Whatever that meant.

In fact, said Max, they were planning to mold Jax into a brainiac supersoldier.

It was nothing new; they'd practically made a habit of it in the previous century, according to Max—for example with mind-altering drugs in the Vietnam War.

"Come on," Cara had said. "Get serious. Jax the Terminator? His biceps are smaller than mine!"

"They are *not*," Jax had squeaked, and lifted his arm up to make a muscle.

It looked pale and flimsy, not unlike a frog's leg.

Max patted him on the head.

"It's OK, small dude," he said. "These days the wars are mostly fought by geeks like you, on computers."

"I'll definitely take a pass on the supersoldier option," said Jax.

"But maybe you won't be *able* to," said Max. "You feel me? Mind control. Electric wires into your eyeballs. Stuff like that. Did you ever see *Clockwork Orange*?"

Jax shook his head.

"It's not exactly PG," conceded Max. "Word to the wise: once they've got you cornered in their high-tech facility, all bets are off. You might come back to us with a chip in your head that communicates with NORAD Central Command."

"What's norad?" asked Cara.

Jax rolled his eyes at Max's dire warnings and went off the next morning anyway, though Cara heard him asking their dad a few faintly anxious questions as they packed his bags into the back of their new used Subaru.

The people at the Advancement Institute couldn't know that Jax could read minds (*ping* them, as he and Cara called it; Max preferred not to discuss it). The Sykes kids kept that one to themselves, although their mother understood. It was even a secret from their father. All that the Institute people knew—Jax claimed and Cara hoped—was that he had a photographic memory and "accelerated learning skills."

Still, Cara was worried that with all their prying and testing, they'd find out about Jax's hidden abilities and the whole thing would turn into a circus. Before they knew it Jax would be kidnapped and locked up in a secret compound at an *undisclosed location*. "Some hyped-up ESP freak show," as Max had helpfully put it.

But Jax had promised he wouldn't let anyone else find out about the pinging.

3

Their mother knew. But she didn't really count.

And, of course, she was gone.

So now the raking of leaves fell to Cara. It'd had to wait for the weekend, because on weekdays she was busy with swim team, debate, and even the annoying dance committee, which her best friend Hayley had forced her to join. Hayley, who lived a few doors down, was intent on becoming popular ("So what? It's a value.") and chose her extracurriculars based on what she saw as their status with the in crowd. Debate team, for instance, got a two out of ten. Not good. Hayley would have stopped Cara from debating at all, if she could. And probably from all activities requiring an IQ score above moron.

Hayley was smart, but she didn't like to admit it in public.

This afternoon Max had gone out with his girlfriend, Zee, and Cara's dad, who taught religious history, was hunkered down in his study writing a paper about some medieval guy who wore scratchy shirts for the glory of God. The professor loved those old-fashioned kooks. He used to teach at Harvard, taking the ferry in from Provincetown three days a week, but he'd gone on sabbatical from there to turn some of his writings on medieval God fans into a book, and as a favor to some other professor was teaching a class at 4 C's in the meantime. In the four months since Cara's mother had been gone, he'd thrown himself into his work even more than usual. He slept on the couch in his study and sometimes got up and paced in the middle of the night, drinking instant coffee that tasted, as far as Cara could tell, like an old shoe.

True, he was slightly more cheerful about the situation since Cara had told him she'd talked to her mom on the phone—but only slightly. Obviously there was still plenty for him to worry about. But at least he was reassured that his wife wasn't hurt or kidnapped or wanting a divorce (as the police had seemed to think).

What had really happened was far more complicated, and the kids had decided to keep it to themselves. Max didn't approve of keeping the truth from their dad, but their mother had asked them to, and in the end even Max had grudgingly agreed. What had *happened* was this: at the beginning of September they'd talked to their mother once, in the backyard, in the middle of the night, before she flew off into the sky. And the last time they saw her she was rising over the ocean on the back of a beast Jax said looked like a pterosaur—which should have been extinct for about sixty-five-million years.

Later he'd looked it up and claimed it fit the profile of a *Quetzalcoatlus northropi*, the only ancient winged reptile he figured might have been big enough to carry a full-grown adult. But "the data were insufficient," as he put it.

Cara thought of that part as something she'd dreamed. It was just easier.

Back then her mother had claimed Cara had the gift of "vision," that she could see what other people couldn't. Cara wasn't so sure, though in the summer she *had* felt she was getting glimpses of hidden things once or twice. And after her mother went away again—and their old dog, Rufus, fell in battle—Cara had made a conscious effort not to think about the war she'd said was coming, *not* to think about the hidden world that lay beneath the visible one. She'd tried to forget the Pouring Man who had attacked them, with water from nowhere coursing steadily down his white face. The beginning of the new school year had been a great distraction, and she'd pushed the summer to the back of her mind—the summer and the dark clouds gathering.

But over the past few days she'd started to feel restless, and sometimes, when Hayley droned on about dances or clothes, her thoughts drifted. Maybe it was just that she wasn't distracted by the newness of school anymore. She knew the routine: she had swim team early in the mornings, then homeroom, then three classes and a spare before lunch, then forty minutes eating at the corner table in the cafeteria with Hayley and her other best friend, Jaye, before her afternoon classes started; it was predictable and unsurprising.

Or maybe she was impatient for Jax to come home. The brainiac boot camp was probably good for him—maybe he was meeting other smart kids and not feeling like such an oddball for once. He'd been adopted when he was two and Cara was five, so she could barely remember life without him; but Jax was so different, with his abilities, that she always worried about him feeling like the odd one out.

Anyway, it *was* a good idea for him to connect with other kids; she knew that. Outside the family, he had only one real friend: Kubler, another high-IQer in Jax's grade. She'd wondered what kind of parent would name their kid Kubler—until she met Kubler's parents. The entire family was a card-carrying dweebfest, each one more socially inept than the last. They were tall, skinny, and gawky as ostriches. The dad was a nerd cliché: he sported toes that turned inward and actually wore terrycloth tennis sweatbands in daily life, right smack around the middle of his forehead. The mom, a math whiz, had giant buckteeth, wore stretchy pants, and had won a famous prize for geniuses that always seemed to make Cara's father grumble. The parents got agitated when Cara tried to say hello and always shepherded Kubler into their aging Volvo without much conversation. But still, she liked them.

Anyway, with Jax and her mom both gone and Max out practically all the time with Zee, the house was depressingly empty. She had Hayley and Jaye, but at the end of the day they went home to their own families, even if those families got on their nerves half the time. Hayley had her doting mom and some cousins who lived in Hyannis and came out on weekends; Jaye had her parents and a little sister in kindergarten who worshiped her.

Whereas Cara...well, lately she sometimes felt, in the empty house, that she hardly had a family at all.

Plus, she'd been having nightmares. They woke her up in the small hours of the morning, but once she was awake, she couldn't remember their details at all and it was hard to get back to sleep. Then all day long she felt there was something she should remember, a forgotten thing that might be important hovering just out of view.

She trudged into the dingy garage and grabbed a trash-can, which she dragged along the driveway of broken white seashells, making an abrasive noise as the can bumped over the shells with its hard, black-plastic wheels. Just as she laid it down in a corner of the yard and started raking in some maple leaves, her cell rang.

"Max should be doing that," said Hayley, when Cara hit answer.

"Doing what?" asked Cara.

"The yard work," said Hayley, and Cara looked up to see she was standing not ten feet away.

Hayley grinned and flipped her pink phone closed. She lived four houses down the street and was a chronic cell-phone abuser.

"Gotta use all those free weekend minutes," she said by way of explanation.

"Free except for the tumor you're going to get in your head from using that thing 24-7, you mean," said Cara.

"Hey, if I'm gonna die for something, it might as well be, like, *communicating* too much with my fellow humans," said Hayley. "Sue me."

"You just give, give, give," said Cara.

That was an expression Hayley's mom liked to use. "I give, give, give," she'd say, sighing. "I'm a giver."

"So is it crazy warm out or what? I mean, it's almost November!"

"If you're going to stand there doing nothing, you could always help me," said Cara, turning back to her pile of leaves.

"Are you kidding? Max gets to go out with that Zee chick, and then I have to grub around in the dirt while they're out there living it up?"

Hayley had had a crush on Max forever, even though she was almost three years younger than he was.

"Zee's nice," said Cara. "You'd like her if you gave her a chance."

"Um, she's my mortal enemy," said Hayley. "I don't *want* to like my enemy. That's the whole point of *having* one."

Cara thought about some quote her dad liked to use— keep your friends close and your enemies closer, or something. Actually, she didn't get it.

"So listen," said Hayley. "You want to do some wardrobe planning with me?"

"Uh, no?"

"For the trip!"

They had their first away-meet of the season tomorrow, a regional that would take the swim team to Boston. They'd get to miss two days of classes.

"OK, then here's my wardrobe planning," said Cara. "Jeans and sweaters."

"You can help *me*, then," said Hayley. "I mean, we're going to the big city. People have style there, Cara. You have to outdress the Joneses."

"In *Boston*? You told me it was the worst-dressed major city on the East Coast!"

"We don't live in the USA anymore, babe. We live on the *internet*."

Hayley had recently told the school's guidance counselor that, for her career, she planned to be a celebrity. Since they'd just started eighth grade, they all had to have a meeting with the counselor, a pasty lady who wore glasses and blobby orange earrings that looked like her kid had made them out of Model Magic. She favored multiple-choice questionnaires and made the students write out their "Interests and Goals" on a long, annoying form. It bore headings like GOALS FOR THIS YEAR. LONG-TERM GOALS.

Cara felt like saying, Hey. I'm in eighth grade here! So under LONG-TERM GOALS she'd just written *TBA*.

But Hayley didn't suffer from those doubts. On her questionnaire, which she filled out at the lunch table sitting at Cara's elbow, she'd written *Celebrity/Pop Star/Actress*.

Hayley wasn't stuck up; she just knew what she wanted. Anyone could do it, she said. It was a matter of willpower. And luck.

Currently, however, her plans for fame were being flouted. In fact, she didn't personally "live on the internet" at all. Her mom wouldn't even let her onto basic social networking sites due to their being the *gateway*, as she put it, to molesters, abductors, and general perverts.

"Oh, fine," sighed Hayley finally, and stooped down to hold the trash can steady on its side so that Cara could rake the leaves in. "But after this, seriously. Let's go to my room, and I'll do a runway walk for you. You can rate my outfits."

"Big thrills."

⚏

That night dinner was just Cara, Max, and her dad, and Max was fifteen minutes late. He came banging through the front door and when he sat down at the table Cara could see he had a hickey on his neck.

Gross.

Or, as Jax would say, because he talked like their dad, "unsavory."

She *did* like Zee, but the thought of how the mark got there was disgusting anyway. How did Zee not get grossed out by Max, too? He picked the wax from his ears right in public. And scrutinized it.

She glanced at her dad to see if he'd noticed. But luckily for her older brother, it wasn't the kind of thing their dad would ever pay attention to.

"Tardy again, Max," he said, and lifted his wine glass. "This is becoming a habit."

"Sorry," said Max, and reached for a roll. Recently most of their dinners were prepared by Lolly, an older lady who often brought her toddler grandson along; tonight she'd served the square dinner rolls you bought unbaked in white cardboard trays at the Stop & Shop. Max could eat about eight of them in a row, so it was fortunate they came by the dozen.

11

"Next time make sure you're here at six on the dot," said their dad sternly.

"Yes, sir," said Max, only half joking.

"So, Cara," said her father. "I understand you're getting on a bus tomorrow morning with the swim team. You'll be away through Tuesday?"

"We're coming back Wednesday morning," said Cara. "Then we go to school for the rest of the day like usual. So I'll be home Wednesday night."

"Zee's going, too," said Max to their dad. "She's one of the best on the team at the hundred I.M."

"I.M.," mused their dad, lifting his fork to his mouth and looking preoccupied. The way he said it, it sounded like he thought it was a foreign language.

"Individual medley?" said Cara.

"Ah," said their dad, and nodded sagely to suggest he'd already known.

Cara remembered watching the Beijing Olympics a few years back; her dad had put his feet up in an armchair nearby and buried his nose in a thick book about the trial of Joan of Arc. He'd grumbled that spectator sports were "… primitive rituals. In the days of the Roman empire, in the games at the Coliseum, tens of thousands watched greedily as slaves tore each other limb from limb."

She wasn't sure what that had to do with Michael Phelps.

"So what's your event, Car?" asked Max.

"I'm just on a relay, is all," said Cara. She wasn't a star swimmer or anything; she just liked being in the water, which always made her feel calm. "Hayley's doing one of the big races, though. She qualified for freestyle."

"Huh. Who knew," said Max.

Hayley didn't practice too hard, but she had natural speed. Freestyle was the most competitive of all.

"And who'll be chaperoning?" asked their dad.

Ever since Max had his car accident while their dad was away at a conference, he worried more than he used to about adult supervision. Although the other kids knew it hadn't been Max's fault at all.

"Hayley's mom's taking time off the hair salon so she can go with us."

Hayley had *not* been happy about that. *Anyone* else's parent was a better option, according to her, even Mr. Abboud, who thought girls shouldn't go out of their houses without scarves covering their heads. Hayley's mom was divorced and, since Hayley was an only child, tended to focus on her a lot. Hayley had made her promise not to hover.

"Don't be a smother mother," she'd said severely, right in front of Cara.

Her mom smiled brightly, flecks of fuchsia-colored lipstick on her teeth.

"Don't stress, honeypie," she said. "If you want to *flirt* with the *boys*, I won't get in your way. As long as there's no *kissing* and you stick to the *curfew*, I'll be practically *invisible*."

Hayley cringed visibly at the word *kissing*. "You better," she said darkly.

Later she told Cara, "Just her *saying* flirt and kiss makes me want to *actually vom*."

Now Cara looked over at her dad, who was just putting down his fork.

"And is Jaye going, too?" he asked.

"Yeah, she's an alternate," said Cara.

"Good, good. Nice girl."

Parents always liked Jaye; they rolled their eyes at Hayley, but Jaye, who had good grades and a neat, polite way about her, got smiles and pats on the back.

"So, Max, you're on dish duty," he went on, pushing his plate away and looking at his watch. "It's time for me to check in with your brother."

They skyped Jax at the Institute at the same time every night to make sure he was OK. It had taken a lot of cajoling from the Institute people to persuade her dad to let Jax go there in the first place, especially during the school year.

"I'll make the call," said Cara.

She often emailed Jax, but she hadn't checked her inbox today and anyway it would be good to see him.

A few minutes later she was in front of the laptop in her bedroom, an old one of Jax's that he'd set up for her. Her dad didn't bother with computers except when he had to, so he pulled up a chair as she clicked on Jax's name and waited for him to answer.

His face filled the screen, peering at them. It was blurry and a little fish-eyed.

"Good Lord, Jackson, move *back*," said her dad irritably. "You're far too close."

Their father took technology as a personal offense. Occasionally he consented to use it, but then, when it wasn't perfect, he acted like it was basically *their* fault. As far as he was concerned, they'd personally invented the microchip.

Jax moved back a little; there was a delay and his image blurred. Still, Cara could see right away that something was wrong.

"So how's it going?" asked their dad.

"OK, I guess," said Jax, and started to drone on instantly about some programming they were having him do, glitches in software, blah blah blah. Cara's dad nodded but was already distracted; Cara noticed he checked his watch in record time. If there was anything the professor enjoyed less than using technology, it was hearing people talk about it.

And then she realized: this was Jax's crafty way of getting rid of him.

"Mm-hmm, sounds good, sounds good," said their dad when there was a pause in Jax's monologue. "And how are the meals going? Did they feed you that boring oatmeal again today?"

Jax shrugged, nodded, and kept talking so tediously about computers that Cara was impressed. Even she had no idea what he was saying; she figured she had to wait it out.

"Well, sorry, kids," said their dad in a fake regretful tone after about another minute of this. "I think I need to get back to the flagellants. You two go ahead though," he said generously, flapping his hand as he stood up. "Talk for as long as you want."

"Er, yeah, thanks, Dad," said Cara.

He didn't get that Skype was free.

"Jackson—same time tomorrow?"

"Sure, Dad," said Jax, and nodded with an impatience Cara thought had to be obvious.

But their dad didn't notice, just tipped an imaginary hat at the computer and closed Cara's bedroom door behind him.

"Smooth, Jax," said Cara.

"Listen," he said, and as he looked around, his image moved slowly, then froze before it started to move again. His voice dropped to a whisper. "There's something wrong here."

"I can't really hear you," said Cara. "If you're worried about someone hearing you, can you just email me or text or something?"

Jax's ESP wasn't a long-distance talent. He had to be near you to know what you were thinking.

"I can't *read* them," he went on, stage-whispering. "That's the first thing. I mean, the other kids, I can. They're normal kids, basically. Smart but normal. But not the people in charge. I can't read them at *all*."

"So—so what does that mean?" asked Cara.

"There are only two people I've met before that I couldn't really read," said Jax. "One's Mom. The other was… *him*."

He meant the Pouring Man—the elemental, as their mother had called him, who had come after them.

"You think the people there are—"

"No. They're not like him," said Jax. He was forgetting to whisper now. "They don't feel dead, or whatever that was—non-living. They're human and all, but I just can't read them. It's like there's a barrier there. I can't trust them, Cara. *I don't trust them.*"

"Well, then come *home!*" said Cara, and felt pumped. She imagined their house with more lamps on, more talking, the warmth of company. "Tell Dad you want to! He'll drive right over the bridge after class tomorrow and get you."

"But that's the other thing," said Jax. "I found out something. And I think I have to stay a while longer. Because I need to find out more."

"*What?* What'd you find out?"

Behind Jax, in the rectangular field that was covered by his laptop's camera, a door opened in stop-action slow motion.

"Jax? ...ight meeting...rec room," said the small, dark head of another kid. It was too far away for the mic to pick up. Then the door closed again, and the head was gone.

"Remember that research material of Mom's?" Jax asked. "On how the oceans are turning more acid? You know—her data that got stolen? I was doing some investigating. I mean, I don't have the information itself or anything, but I was looking at some old work emails of hers. I got them off her iPad. And I found a conversation she was having with another scientist that suggested her info wasn't just the pH-level data other researchers have. What it looked like to me was, Mom found a *major unknown source.*"

"Source of what?"

"Greenhouse gas," whispered Jax. "*Shooting into the ocean.* That's what makes the seawater acid, right? Our factories spew all those gases into the air, and they go into the ocean, among other places, and the ocean stores them. But the problem is, the more of those global-warming gases the ocean stores, the more acid the water is getting. See?"

"Sort of."

"Most of the pollution comes from cars and planes and power plants, right? Us burning coal and oil and gas. But the point is: Mom found another source. A source that isn't any of those. *Another place the gases are coming from.*"

The door opened behind him again. This time the head that stuck through the crack was larger and higher off the ground. An adult. It wore black-framed glasses.

"Jax! We're waiting," said the head.

"OK," said Jax cheerfully. "Just talking to my big sister!"

"Talk later," said the head sternly, and disappeared. But the door stayed open.

"Gotta go," said Jax, dropping his cute-kid smile and sinking back to a stage whisper. "The key is this, Car: I think she *did* discover something unique. Something that's not widely known. This *source.* And I need to find out what it is. And where."

"OK. Well, so—but why do you have to do it *there*?"

"Better computing power. Faster connections, more access. I *have* to. Trust me. OK. Oops, gotta book."

And then he was gone, replaced by a small icon on Cara's empty screen.

---

Getting ready for bed after she finished packing for the trip, Cara decided the chaos in her room had finally gotten out of hand. These days, when she or Max or Jax *did* consent to tidy up, it was usually only because Lolly was threatening to use her powerful vacuum to suck their personal belongings off the floor, never to be seen again.

Lolly did a little housework, but she concentrated on the first floor and usually came into the kids' bedrooms only when (as she put it) she was forced to.

Cara started to pick up her room by the soft orange light of her old bedside lamp, patterned with seashells and starfish. Her mother had bought it for a dollar from a motel that was going out of business. The briny smell of the ocean wafted in a half-open window, mixed in with the faint bayside odor of fishy things—probably horseshoe crabs in mid-decay. She lifted clothes off the floor, straightened her desk and closet, then decided she could even change her sheets.

Hey, once every few months, why not?

After she pulled back the flowery turquoise coverlet and the jumble composed of the top sheet and blankets, she also lifted her pillow, and there, lying on the bottom sheet, was a small, blue eye on a silver band. Her favorite ring, a good-luck charm made of blown glass that her mother had given her. A *nazar*, they called them in Turkey, to ward off the evil eye—a good eye to ward off evil ones. She'd been missing it since the summer, and it'd been here all the time.

*Huh*, she thought, and picked the ring up to slide it back onto her finger. She thought ruefully of the fairy tale about the princess who slept on a pile of twelve mattresses and could still feel the tiny pea beneath. *Not much of a princess, am I?*

She found she was thinking of Jax again and what he had said about their mother's work: a source, *an unknown source*. Where and what could this source be? And what did it have to do with what had happened to them in August?

Her fingers still held the ring, settled now in its famil-iar place. Without knowing how she'd gotten there, she was lying on her bed—aware of her grimy sheets, the usual few grains of beach sand at the bottom—but she wasn't seeing her room anymore. She was shifting through the turquoises and blues of her covers without touching anything, and in front of her was darkness, and out of the darkness came bubbling, roiling black columns of what looked like smoke.

The smoke was dispersing strangely—through water, she thought, not air. It must be water.

The black clouds were coming out of bumpy black and brown and white chimneys, not manmade but maybe min-eral, she guessed—towers jutting out of rock piles on what she thought must be the seabed. The black smoke came billowing out of these rough castle-like pillars—billowing and billowing in clouds that spread and bubbled up again until she felt hypnotized watching it.

But then she was moving closer to the rocks, right up to the towers and into the dark of the smoke and then emerging from it on the other side. There were tubelike creatures capped with plumes of red; there were lit-up floating animals that reminded her of shrimp. Others looked like jellyfish, and others, yet, the single-celled organisms she'd seen in biology class. They swirled around her until she passed them, too, and went farther down, burrowing through the ocean floor. Then it was black again and she couldn't see anything for a while—until she could.

She could see, but she couldn't understand. There was movement here, there were spaces—caverns maybe?—and streaks of light through the darkness like rivers of fire, she thought, but it was all too surreal; she couldn't see much beyond the blurs and flashes. She felt as though she were inside a volcano. Then she saw a line in front of her, an impossibly sharp, vertical line of gray, unlike anything else, that held her gaze. It was something recognizable, though she couldn't put her finger on it....

But she was in her bedroom again. Her old, familiar bedroom with its cozy disorder. She was sitting upright in a pile of rumpled bed linens, feeling a little dizzy. Outside she heard the crickets, the faint rhythmic wash of the tide. A low drumbeat from Max's room, where he was listening to music without his headphones.

She held up her finger, still faintly tanned from the summer, with its short, chewed nail and the blue-and-white nazar ring.

Definitely not a coincidence.

She'd mislaid the ring after what happened in August; now that she thought about it, she'd had no visions since then. Not a single one, at least that she remembered.

Until now.

Although…maybe the nightmares had been pieces of visions, trying to come through.

Not that she knew what she'd seen. But it had been a glimpse into *something*. She hadn't made it up.

And that meant the ring had to have powers: her mother had given her a talisman, not just a good-luck charm. She'd suspected before, but she hadn't known for sure. In a way, she thought curiously, she hadn't wanted to know. In a way, she had ignored the evidence.

The vision had to have something to do with Jax's theory about her mother's discovery, the so-called source. Which she'd been thinking about when she slid the ring onto her finger. That wasn't a coincidence, either.

It was all starting again, she thought, and felt the tiny hairs lift along her arms. She didn't know whether to feel excited or stubbornly rooted to the ground.

It wasn't that regular life fell away; it was that new elements appeared without warning.

It was the possible, opening up in midair.

## Two

*Clothing-stuffed backpack over her shoulder, Cara rang* Hayley's doorbell for her ride to school. There they would get on the charter bus that would take the team onto the mainland and finally into Boston.

It was so early it was dark out, with the first pale streaks in the sky; Cara was still rubbing the sleep from her eyes when Hayley's mother answered the door with her lips lined in purple and her hair done up in a sixties beehive.

Hayley's mom ran a beauty salon along Route 6, a salon with a lot of fake flowers in it where young women got their nails done and old ladies got their hair washed a lavender color and set into wavy helmets. Cara and Hayley had asked her what the reason was behind that old-lady blue hair situation, but Mrs. M never explained it too well. It seemed like a ritual from ancient times—the equivalent of a secret handshake. In any case, Mrs. Moore's own hair was always elaborate and tacky, like a Gaga wig but maybe without the irony.

"Come on in, Cara, hon!" she enthused in her Georgia accent.

It turned *on* into *own* and *in* into *Ian*. Come own Ian!

"Thanks," said Cara.

Hayley's mom often made Cara feel a bit embarrassed—though not as embarrased as Hayley felt. Mrs. M. was nice, no argument there, but she was also shiny and loud and stood too near, where Cara's mother was soft-spoken and, like a chameleon, always seemed to match wherever she found herself.

"Would you go on up and get her, sweetcakes? I'll be waiting out in the car," said Mrs. M, and pulled on a lumpy fur jacket Cara really hoped was fake. It had animal tails dangling.

Cara dropped her bags and took the stairs two at a time. Hayley was one of those people who always made you wait—at least, if she was involved in a momentous decision such as what to wear. In restaurants, she was the one still studying the menu when everyone else already had a plate in front of them.

"Hay! Time to go!" called Cara as she swung past the shag-carpeted landing and into the upstairs hallway.

Hayley's door was open, showing a wall of celebrity collages. She cut up the gossip and fashion magazines her mom's clients left in the salon.

"I'm coming! Geez," said Hayley.

In fact, she wasn't coming at all. She was posing in front of her full-length mirror, admiring herself in a leisurely fashion and rocking an eighties outfit. She had feathery earrings dangling from her ears and an asymmetrical, triangle-shaped coat that looked, to Cara, on the ugly side.

Of course, she would never say that to Hayley. It wasn't that Hay's feelings would be hurt or anything. Far from it.

She'd just roll her eyes at Cara's poor fashion sense and give her a lecture on glamor and trends and the importance of retro. But Cara also knew that Hay's elaborate outfits were carefully chosen at thrift stores. They didn't have the money for brand-new clothes.

"We have to *go* now," said Cara. "It's a bus. Not a personal taxi service."

"So my goal is like an early Madonna, sleazy gutterslag kinda look," said Hayley.

"Nice," nodded Cara. "Yeah. I can see that. But let me ask you this. Did you pack your swimsuit?"

Hayley stopped popping her gum and snapped her fingers. She swished by Cara, down the hall to the bathroom (where everything was fluffy and/or made of conch shells and beach glass and a really bad poster showed two sets of footprints turning to one in the sand, along with some motto about Jesus carrying you) and grabbed a threadbare Speedo dangling off the shower rod.

"Good thought. Kudos," she said.

⧯

By the time they were getting into the car, Hayley was already irritated with her mom, who proceeded to grill them all the way to school—driving, as usual, like she was under the influence though all she was drinking was coffee—on the names and family histories of other kids on the team. Mrs. M was what you might call an extrovert. Extreme. She was sure to talk to everyone and bustle around everywhere, Cara thought. There was no way she'd fly under the radar.

"Rule Number One," said Hayley as they pulled into the parking lot. "If you absolutely *have* to talk to people, at least do me one favor. Or all my work on the popularity situation will be wrecked. Do *not* constantly remind people you're my mother. In fact, if you don't refer to it a single time, that'd be awesome."

"*Hay*ley!" chided her mother with a smile, as though her daughter was joking.

"Keep the relationship, like, under wraps," said Hayley as they pulled into a parking space. "Because if you keep trying to tell *humiliating* baby stories about me, I'll have to end my suffering. All your years of bringing me up will be totally wasted in a tragic teen suicide."

"Honey, people already *know* I'm your mama," protested Mrs. M. "I mean"—*Ah main*—"I hate to break it to you, but that little kitty's already out of the bag."

"What I'm *saying* is, don't rub it *in*," said Hayley. "Let them forget a bit. You know what I'm saying?"

She popped her door open and shrugged her miniature backpack over her shoulders.

"Hi, guys," said Jaye as Hayley plucked her larger bag from the trunk.

Jaye was Asian-looking from her mother's side, pretty and slim; she stood with her duffel bag placed neatly on the ground beside her, light-blue iPod buds in her ears. Jaye could be timid, unlike Hayley; she was comfortable with her two best friends but not too great at reaching out to other, new people.

But what all the approving parents didn't know—when they patted her on the back to reward her for being an A student and also for not wearing shiny purple lip gloss like Hayley—was how independent she could be, despite the shyness. She was the type you could depend on to know things like CPR without ever bragging about it. Recently she'd tried out for the school play because her mother had thought it would be a good way to conquer her shyness; she'd done it even though it terrified her, and she'd gotten a small role.

Her parents were well-dressed and reserved: her dad was an engineer, and her mother ran a plant nursery. Compared to Mrs. M, Jaye's parents were distinctly unembarrassing.

"God, you're *so* lucky to be solo," said Hayley, apparently thinking the same thing. "I still can't believe my mom's tagging along. I'm having orphan fantasies."

"Well," said Jaye, and shrugged, "if you ignore them for long enough, sometimes they go away."

She and Hayley laughed, and then stopped and both looked at Cara guiltily.

"Oh, wow," said Jaye. "Slowly remove foot from mouth. I'm *so* sorry."

"It's all right," said Cara softly.

And it was true. It had been harder to hear things like that before she saw her mother and was reassured that she hadn't left them—or not because she wanted to, anyway.

Not that Cara didn't struggle with her absence. But at least it hadn't been caused by something that was wrong with their family. Hayley knew what had happened, too—that Cara's mother was out there fighting in some mysterious war, and had visited them; that there were *more things in heaven and earth, Horatio, than are dreamt of in your philosophy*…(Max, usually a so-so student, had a thing for Shakespeare quotes).

But Jaye didn't know any of that. Cara and her brothers had talked to Hayley about it, and they'd all agreed not to say anything to anyone else—or not yet, anyway. The true story was too far-fetched, and Max, in particular, wanted to limit how many people heard it. Jaye's family had been away in Maine when the whole thing went down, and as far as she knew, Cara's mother had left back in June, and that was that.

Coach Essick was herding people into the charter bus, a tall black behemoth with a bright purple swipe on the side. The coach was a beefy bald guy who liked his swimmers to say daily affirmations.

"I'm a win, win, winner!" he said now, pumping a hairy arm. "Let's hear it!"

"…uh yeah, winner," mumbled one of the guys, half-asleep and sheepish.

The affirmations weren't always a big hit.

"In you get, girls!" said Mrs. M in her too-perky voice.

About an hour later the bus was crossing the bridge to the mainland, an educational video about reptiles playing on the TV monitor. Hayley was talking to older kids near the rear of the bus, at what she considered a minimum safe distance from her mother; Cara and Jaye were getting ahead on their homework in a seat near the front.

The text alert on Cara's phone went off. Jax.

FOUND SOURCE, read the text.

*Wht source?* she typed back.

"*Lizards are robust, adaptive creatures...,*" droned the British narrator.

No reply.

He was probably busy.

She put her phone away.

"*...but, due to global warming, at least 40 percent of the world's lizard populations are expected to go extinct by the year 2080. Overall, if current emissions trajectories persist, one-quarter to one third of all the world's species are projected to disappear by century's end.*"

"That's really scary," said Jaye quietly.

Cara looked into her friend's eyes. It was good to have Jaye beside her; Jaye understood a few things that Cara really worried about but Hayley didn't seem to be interested in.

"I *know*," she said.

"Hey, Cara!"

It was Zee, Max's girlfriend, leaning out of her seat a few rows back.

"Hi, Zee," said Cara, twisting around.

"Max said to keep an eye on you," smiled Zee.

"Huh," said Cara. "Thanks, but…there are kind of a lot of babysitters around here already."

They both glanced up to where Mrs. M was standing in the aisle and leaning over the double seat that held Coach Essick and Mr. Abboud. She stuck one hip out, swirled her egregious Garfield keychain on an index finger, and chattered gaily to the two men as Coach Essick grinned and nodded and Mr. Abboud stared miserably out his filmy window.

The poor guy had to avert his eyes, Cara realized: not only was Mrs. M not wearing a headscarf, but she was showing major tanned, freckled *cleave*, as Hayley would put it if she noticed. Cara didn't know whom to feel bad for— Mr. Abboud, Hayley, or Mrs. M herself.

"See what you mean," said Zee. She smiled again, and Cara thought she could see why Max liked her so much. There was a warmth to Zee—an easy friendliness. "But just so you know, I'm here if you need anything."

"Thanks," said Cara.

Her phone buzzed, so she turned around again, slipping it out of her backpack pocket.

Another text from Jax.

WHERE R U?

*Sagamore Brij.*

She waited till an answer came up.

COME GET ME.

Oh *no*, she thought. Now?
*On bus!* she typed. *Y? HOW?*
SCARED TELL NO 1 PLZ COME!

She spent the rest of the bus trip using her cell to figure out how to get to the Institute from the hotel, then from the big school where they were going to be competing. The team had its first races this afternoon, and she was supposed to be there, of course; but she wasn't slated to be *in* any of today's races unless someone swimming the backstroke fell violently ill. The relay wasn't until tomorrow—heats in the morning, finals in the afternoon if the team made the cut. Maybe, she thought, just maybe she could slip out without anyone noticing once they were all sitting there in the bleachers—at least, if people were focused on watching the races.

Distraction was the only way. If she distracted Mrs. M, she thought, she could do it. She'd *have* to distract her, because Mrs. M was directly assigned to her and Jaye and Hayley, among others. Cara could sneak out and get on the subway—it looked like there was a T station a few blocks from the host school, and then it was only a couple of stops from there to the Institute. She could take the T by herself—she'd taken it before, though admittedly with her mother or her dad—and go find Jax and bring him with her. Maybe she'd take him back to the meet; maybe she'd send him to the hotel room she'd be sharing with Hayley and Jaye. She'd work that part later.

31

But she was going to need Hayley's help, she realized, if she wanted to get away with it. There was no way Mrs. M would give her permission to take off. Ever since her divorce, she didn't even let Hayley walk around the neighborhood by herself, much less get on a public transit system in a city of millions. She was obsessed with true-crime shows and seemed to watch in morbid fascination when it was a show about a missing kid.

When the bus pulled into the parking lot of the hotel—a blocky place with not a single tree or bush in sight—and Mr. Abboud went to get them checked in, Cara waited till Mrs. M was busy flirting with Coach Essick again, then got out of her seat and went to the back of the bus to talk to Hayley, in the very last row.

She murmured in Hayley's ear about Jax, about how she needed a distraction so she could get away.

"Oh *no*," Hayley groaned. "The Sykes family drama strikes back! I don't want anything to *do* with my mom at the meet, and now you're telling me you want me to, like, try to get her *attention*? Just because your little brother is *homesick*?"

"It's not just homesick, it's—"

"But Car, come *on*! And plus I have a *race* today!"

Cara bit her lip. It was true: not only was Hayley racing in a couple of hours, but this was her worst social nightmare. She didn't know what she'd been thinking; she could almost kick herself.

Maybe…maybe she could ask Jaye? Normally she wouldn't, because Jaye was too shy to do anything that would draw attention to herself—Cara always thought of Hayley when she thought of drama. But *maybe*...after all, Jaye had had the guts to try out for the play when her mother encouraged her to; she was trying to conquer her shy streak. Cara went back up front, to where her friend was still typing away studiously on her laptop.

"Jaye? I was wondering if maybe you could help me," she whispered.

⚅

It was during a lull between races, the fifty-meter fly and the backstroke, that Jaye made her move.

Cara never saw it begin, but all of a sudden, a little ways down the bleachers, Mrs. M was comforting Jaye as she pretended to cry, whimpering something about not being smart enough. It was a bit of a stretch since Jaye was a solid A student, but Mrs. M had a soft spot for kids with anxiety, so Cara had figured it might work on Hayley's mom.

She felt a little guilty thinking like that, having to trick Mrs. M, but there was just no other way. Jax didn't have a mother like Mrs. M around to obsessively nurture him right now. All he had was Cara.

Then the harsh beep of the starting gun blared; the swimmers splashed off the blocks. There was an instant noisewall of cheers and yells, so deafening it was hard to think. She seized her opportunity, slipping behind Mrs. M and an eye-rolling Jaye and heading for the locker room. (Hayley had agreed to keep an eye on things, and if she had to she was going to tell her mother Cara was in a bathroom stall throwing up.) She'd stashed her backpack in an empty locker a few minutes before; now she went through the shower room and swung by to bang open the locker door and grab it. She was nervous, she realized, her stomach flip-flopping: maybe the sickness would turn out not to be a lie after all.

She left the changing room and walked down a wide hall of lockers and closed classroom doors, pack over one shoulder, shoes squeaking annoyingly on the linoleum and making her feel like someone was going to hear and come after her. (Even though, in this foreign-feeling school, no one knew her at all outside the cavernous, fluorescent echo chamber of the pool.) Classes were all in session, she guessed, because there was no one in the long hall and teachers' voices droned from behind closed doors.

She set the timer on her phone as she walked, so she could tell at a glance how long she'd been AWOL. Then she pocketed the phone and was outside, the double doors swinging to behind her.

She *never* did things like this. She never played hooky, and she hardly ever lied, except for what her mother called white lies, which were usually just politeness. Or not premeditated, anyway. Plus the subway…she was old enough—*well* old enough, clearly. Thousands of thirteen-year-olds took the T.

Actually it was pathetic to even be worried, she said to herself. It was just that she only came to the city for concerts and museums, mostly—to see *The Nutcracker* at Christmas-time or go into her dad's old office when he was teaching at Harvard or the Museum of Fine Arts when her mother wanted to see paintings. At home she was comfortable getting around by herself because she knew her piece of the Cape like the back of her hand; she'd been practically everywhere on her bike. But that was the laid-back Cape. This was a major city, its long, crowded streets sprawling for miles around her, and here she was a stranger in a strange land.

*Don't be lame*, she told herself out loud.

Then there it was, the sign for the station. She was down the stairs, feeding her dollars into the machine to buy a card; she was checking the map and she was through the turnstile; she was on the platform.

And in fact it was completely mundane. This was the middle of the day, so there weren't any of the bustling, pushy crowds that filled the tunnels at rush hour and used to intimidate her when she was a little kid clinging to her mother's hand. A few people milled around, even a group of kids her own age, mostly guys plus one chunky girl wearing black and pink tights that had a picture of a zipper down the outside of each of her legs. Cara couldn't help staring at the zippers.

The kids were kicking some trash and laughing; some old men sat on benches.

She heard the faint rush of the train, and then it got louder and louder and she was gazing into the yellow glare of its oncoming lights. First she thought she might be hypnotized, and then she stood back—a panic briefly surged up as she remembered stories of people pushed off platforms and into the path of the trains—and was safe. She felt the air rushing past and saw the flickering blur of the side of the cars, one after the other.

She touched the nazar thoughtlessly, turning it on her finger as the silver and red flickering of the cars slowed and the train screeched to a stop. Into the flickering came a line of gray—a solid, straight column of gray, hovering there in front of the blur of the train windows with their rows of seated passengers' heads.

Then it was gone.

As visions went, this one was impressively boring, she thought, and smiled faintly. But it made her think the visions came when she had fingers from *both* hands touching the nazar. When the ring had been beneath her pillow, she'd had nightmares she couldn't really remember. They might or might not have had anything to do with the talisman, since the ring hadn't been touching her skin directly....

She wondered what a vertical gray line could mean. It was the same line she'd seen in her undersea vision, she thought, her vision of the source—had to be.

On the other hand, one gray line looked a lot like the next. Maybe it was more of a glitch than a meaningful part of what she saw, she reflected as the subway train's doors slid open and she stepped in. Like a hair on the film of an

36

old movie, trembling in the light from the projector—something she often noticed when they went to see the vintage B movies her dad liked so much, back when special effects were idiotic looking, when slimy creatures rose groaning from swamps and muscular-looking mummies tottered around in filthy bandages.

That was probably it, she thought: a technical glitch. If technology could have glitches, then surely a vision could. Right?

As the doors closed and the train jerked to a start, she looked around for a subway map, wanting to make sure she knew where she was going. There it was, a couple of benches down: a red, branching line with the stops marked. She walked toward it. Briefly she thought she saw something bright reflected in the dark window of the subway car—something that flickered. But when she turned to look at the spot it might be reflecting from, there was nothing but a nondescript man sitting there beneath the subway map. She couldn't quite make out the words on the map, so she stepped toward it.

"Excuse me," she said, and leaned in a bit to read the names of the stations. Yep: two more stops, and they were already pulling into the first.

She straightened up, noticing for the first time that the car was almost empty. There was only that one man, sitting in front of her. How had that happened? She could have sworn there'd been other people around when she got on; they must have gotten out. The double doors were already closing.

She moved down the car as the train stuttered forward so that she wouldn't be sitting right across from the only other person there; that could be awkward. She sat down at one end of a three-person bench along the train's wall and glanced down at her phone to see if Jax had texted her yet.

No Service, it read.

No reception down here. Made sense.

Then she looked up again.

The man was opposite her. On the bench.

She hadn't heard any footsteps, she was sure, or seen him change seats.

She felt a jolt of fear.

Then again, he wasn't looking at her or anything. He was a youngish guy, maybe in his twenties, with light brown hair and bland, office-type clothing you didn't really notice. He was looking down, consulting a paper in his hand.

It was probably nothing to worry about, she thought.

She looked at the time on her cell. 2:33. She brought up a simple game and played it for a while. The next station was hers, anyway.

But then it turned out not to be a station. Rather, the train was slowing down in the tunnel. Had to be. It slowed down and lurched to a stop.

Her hands, she saw, were trembling slightly.

Nothing to worry about, she repeated to herself. Nothing.

She looked up. Around the train windows was blackness.

The man was still there.

And now he *was* looking at her. Something about his eyes weirded her out, so she looked away quickly.

"Guess we're stuck in—in some kind of delay," she said uncomfortably, to break the tension.

He said nothing.

Maybe he didn't speak English, she thought, or maybe he couldn't hear…but those were just excuses, she thought, and felt more and more anxious. Her pulse was racing. Could you change cars while the train was going? She was almost sure you couldn't. Your leg would get chopped off, or something.

It felt too tense. Plus it was *hot*, she realized, hot and stuffy; there was sweat beading at her temples and along the edge of her hairline. She forced herself to stand up and moved off again toward the front of the car. There was a rectangular window in the door that looked into the next car up; at least if she stood in the window, she guessed, someone might see her, and then the man couldn't do anything.

Right?

Through the window, the next car on the train looked empty. She didn't want to check the back window, because then she'd have to walk past the man again. Acting casual, she sat down on another bench.

Just then—what a relief!—the train made a screeching noise and moved, albeit at a pace that seemed painfully slow. It gained speed. It was way too hot for comfort now, though the heat didn't feel as oppressive when she knew they were getting somewhere again. Her phone said only two minutes had passed—two minutes that had felt like forever.

When she looked up from it, he was there again. Opposite.

*No.*

She looked away quickly, touching her ring in a nervous reflex.

Then his mouth was wide open and flames were roaring within. *Flames.* She jerked back in her seat and banged her head on the wall, her ears ringing. He looked at her without moving, smiling horrifically, and inside his open mouth there were no teeth. No *anything*. Except fire. It was like roaring flames—bright orange and hard to look at....

She jumped up and ran back along the car to the very end, not stopping even to breathe, and banged on the door—there *were* some passengers in the car behind, their eyes cast down as they read books or typed on handhelds, but none of them looked up at her as she banged on the window. Not a single one noticed her there, battering her fists against the Plexiglas panel...and somehow she couldn't say *help*. The word caught in her throat. There wasn't enough breath.

Now the train was slowing down—not another delay? Not another dead stop in the blackness of the tunnel? What would she *do*?

She didn't turn around—wouldn't, *couldn't*—but then she was looking at the window, the heels of her hands still hitting on it weakly, and instead of the passengers in the next car ignoring her, all she saw was him. Standing behind her with his fiery hole of a mouth.

Flames licked and burned in the empty face.

The doors sprang open. She turned to dash past him—fight her way past him if she had to, she was telling herself—but he was gone.

Everyday people were streaming in.

She ran up the many steps, half afraid the man with fire in his mouth was pursuing her, though she didn't exactly feel his presence anymore. Then she was out of the T station, trembling, a sensation of pinpricks on her cheeks and upper arms. She was relieved to be in the fresh, cold air.

Anyway, he was gone, right? He was gone now.

She leaned against a planter on the sidewalk beneath some big trees with dead leaves and tried to slow down her fast breathing. There was a subway map in a big plastic frame nearby, sticking out of the sidewalk; there were trash cans in casings of what looked like nubbly pebbles. It was gray and bleak around here. A few people walked past, but none of them was him.

He was gone.

She pulled out her phone—her heartbeat was still rapid, but she had to do something to occupy her while she calmed down—and brought up the street map with the Institute and the Kendall Square station on it. She had about three blocks to walk; it wasn't complicated. But the Institute itself, Jax had said, was in a building without a name on it, so all she had was numbers: a street address, a floor number, a room number. The kids shared rooms, Jax had said, and there would be a guard at the front desk, and if anyone tried to stop her she was supposed to duck into a stairwell and text him.

No new messages…. Should she call him?

She *should* check in with Hayley; it had been twenty-four minutes since she left the pool. She texted as she walked, asking if Mrs. M had noticed her absence. Not that it would change anything. Just that she might as well know.

Nope J, wrote Hayley.

So she dialed Jax next, still jangling with adrenalin from the memory of those dancing flames in the hole of that mouth…. Could it have been the nazar? Was it just the *ring* that had made her see that?

Maybe the flames hadn't been real at all—a hallucination, a vision about who the guy was. She'd only seen them when she reached down and touched the ring. Before that he'd been just a man, staring. Yes, maybe the ring had put that picture in her head. And the flaming mouth hadn't been real at all.

It was a relief to think so.

On the other end, as she held the phone to her ear and walked, Jax's phone rang and rang and went to voice mail.

The building's number was above its revolving doors in blocky, modern letters. She went into a high-ceilinged lobby with a bright white floor; a fattish security guard sat behind a high counter.

She heard the squeak of her sneakers again as she crossed the linoleum toward him. She was still on edge from what had happened in the T; it made her self-conscious.

"Hi, uh, I'm here to visit someone on the eighth floor? At the Institute for Advancement?" she said.

Jax had said *tell no one*—did that include this guy? And tell no one *what*, anyway? That she was coming to get him? Was she supposed to be sneaking in? But how could she?

No, she thought, he couldn't have meant that.

Anyway the guard barely paid any attention, just waved a dismissive hand in the direction of the elevators and turned a page in his magazine, so she walked past him and pushed the button.

Even on the eighth floor, where the Institute housed its teachers and students, there wasn't much to trumpet what it was. When the elevator doors slid open, all there was to tell her she'd come to the right place was a small plastic sign on the wall. I.A. STES 800-898.

Jax's room was supposed to be 822. She walked along the corridor, watching the numbers on the doors rise.

"Why! If it isn't Cara Sykes!" said a man's voice behind her.

She spun around and saw one of the doors was open; an older guy stood there. He had a salt-and-pepper goatee and wore a suit and a beige winter coat.

"Remember me? I work with your mother!" he said. "Roger!"

"Oh, right," said Cara, relieved.

43

Roger was another marine biologist who did research with her mother at Woods Hole; he studied the ocean, like her mother, and was also a professor. He was her mother's boss, basically, though he never acted bossy.

"But what are you *doing* here?" she asked, and then hoped it didn't seem too rude.

"Oh, I consult," he said. "You know—come in and out, work on a project here and there. I was the one who first told your mother about the Institute's gifted-kid program."

"Oh," said Cara, and nodded.

"You come to see your little brother?" he asked.

"Yeah, I missed him," she said, and smiled casually, she hoped, to indicate it was a routine visit.

"Oh, hey," said Roger, like a light bulb had come on in his head, and reached into a coat pocket. "Would you give him this? It's just a souvenir pen, but he left it in your mother's office a while ago and I happened to notice it there as I was leaving for the city this morning."

It was a cheesy ballpoint pen from the Aquarium, with a big orca bobblehead on the end.

"Uh, sure," said Cara, and took it.

*Random*, she thought. But whatever. Maybe Roger was trying to reach out because he was sorry for them. She didn't think he had kids of his own; he might just be clueless.

"I'll let you get to your visit, then," he said, and patted her shoulder lightly before he ducked down the hall and hit the elevator button. She turned and kept walking down the narrow hall along the row of doors. 814, 816.

He must have gotten tired of waiting for the elevator, because when Cara looked over her shoulder to wave good-bye, she hadn't heard the elevators ding but he was gone anyway: she heard the EXIT door to the stairs click shut.

"Jax?" she said, standing at the door marked 822. She knocked.

The door wasn't locked or even closed all the way; it pushed open on her second knock.

"Jax?" she called more loudly as she stepped in.

There was a wooden bunk bed with colorful quilts on it, a round, warm-yellow throw rug, and two computer setups at desks against the opposite wall; the room was wallpapered especially for geeks, with $E=MC^2$ and other equations printed on it.

She didn't see any geeks around, though.

She could sit down and wait for him, she guessed. She sat down on the bottom bunk. Although…

She flipped the bobblehead pen onto the bedspread beside her and lifted her phone. Forty-three minutes, now, since she'd snuck away from the pool. Still: Hayley or Jaye would text her if there was a problem.

"Cara!" came a hiss from beneath her. She jumped. "Close the door!"

She walked over and closed it. Then Jax's blond head and hands, covered in cobwebs, were sticking out from beneath the bed.

"What are you *doing*, Jax?" she squeaked as he crawled all the way out onto the rug.

"Hiding," said Jax. "Clearly."

He rubbed a cobweb off an eyelid.

"What's going on?" she asked.

"I heard you coming, and I thought you could be one of them."

"One of who?"

"I don't know. I told you. I can't read anyone here. I'm not used to it! How do you go around all the time not knowing what's going on in people's heads?"

He looked off-balance to Cara, on edge in a way she wasn't used to.

"Jax. Welcome to the human race. It's going to be OK."

She reached out and clasped his arm, and slowly he crept up onto the bed and sat beside her. She slung an arm around his shoulders.

"It's OK, Jax. Really."

"I found the source *she* found, and now they're after me. I *know* it," he said, dropping his voice to a whisper. "You have to get me out of here."

"The source?"

"It's over there," he said, pointing. "On my laptop."

"The source?"

"The data! *About* the source. I'll show you at home. But now can we go?"

"Get your stuff, then," said Cara. "Explain it to me later. But Jax, there's something—on my way over here I thought I saw—"

"We have to *sneak* out," interrupted Jax, not listening. "They can't let me go without a parent present."

46

"Well—geez, Jax!" she burst out, impatient. "Why didn't you just call *Dad*, then?"

Forty-seven minutes, said the timer on her phone. And nothing seemed dangerous in this place; so far the best word to describe it was *boring*. Dangerous was *out there*, if it was anywhere. If the man with the flames had been real. Jax was overreacting. And instead of just calling their dad, who could come and pick him up without any stress at all in an actual car, he'd made her stage a prison break and then jump through all these hoops.

Because even assuming it *was* the ring that had made her see flames—and even if, say, the flames were a vision and therefore more a *symbol* for something than real fire—a guy following her around an otherwise empty subway car had been deeply creepy. Plus she'd probably catch some serious flak when she and Jax got back, unless it was in the next half hour or so and the whole thing passed without notice. (Mrs. M, unlike Cara's own parents, was into grounding.) She could even be kicked off the team for this. There were strict rules about how you had to act when you went to meets.

And then there was the issue of what to *do* with Jax now that she had him. Maybe she could still get back before Mrs. M knew she was gone; maybe she could just explain that Jax had missed his family and showed up. Maybe they'd call her dad and it would turn out fine; they'd simply take Jax home with them. There were a bunch of empty seats in the bus, after all.

47

"*Ow!* What's that?" squeaked Jax. He felt beneath his leg on the quilt, pulling out the bobblehead pen. "This thing *scratched* me. Right through my pants!"

"Oh, sorry—Roger gave it to me to give to you," said Cara. "You know. Roger who works with Mom at the—"

She was about to go on when there was a sharp rap on the room door and someone pushed it open without even waiting for a *Come in.*

"Jackson?"

It was a tall, thin woman with an Afro and a foreign accent—she must be one of the teachers—and she looked almost angry.

Was she one of the ones Jax said he couldn't trust?

"Jax, you're supposed to be in session," said the teacher sternly.

Her gaze flicked to Cara, but then she and Cara were both looking at Jax. His *eyes* were odd—almost milky. Almost cloudy.

Cara hadn't noticed it before.

"Mrs. Omotoso, I don't feel so good," he said slowly.

And Cara could see it was true.

Mrs. Omotoso crossed the room quickly and put her slender hand over his forehead.

"Cara, we need to move him right away," she said. "To the infirmary."

It wasn't till later that Cara realized that, at that particular moment, she hadn't yet told the teacher who she was.

## Three

*By the time more of them came to get Jax, his eyes were closed* and his breathing was shallow. His skin was pale in a way that scared Cara.

Two men slid him off the bed and onto the gurney, a slim, sheet-covered cot with wheels that rattled loudly. Then they were headed out of the room and other adults were converging on them. Cara practically had to jog to keep up.

She hustled alongside the gurney as Mrs. Omotoso and the men—other teachers, she guessed—pushed it quickly down the corridor; kids popped their heads out of doors to watch the hurrying crowd pass by. At the end of the hallway the group turned and went into a small elevator, angling the gurney in through the narrow door and squeezing in around it, pressed up against each other and the walls; but just a few moments after it had dinged closed, the elevator door slid open again and the crowd was squeezing out, Cara tripping and righting herself in their wake.

And in an instant the Institute seemed like a whole different place—dimmer, older, softer. In here the corridors were more like tunnels than halls; she thought of the back stairways of medieval castles seen in movies. It was incredible that this ancient-seeming place was part of the generic office building: there was dark wood everywhere, shadowy corners and niches, ornate light fittings on the walls instead of fluorescent tubes on the ceilings. Barely lit alcoves housed statues, large amber-tinted oil paintings, and faded tapestries hung on the walls.

"Where *are* we?" asked Cara, but she was still being rushed along as the teachers concentrated on Jax, whose small, skinny body jiggled inertly as the gurney bumped over the well-worn planks of the floor.

Now the place reminded her of a musty, half-neglected museum, she was thinking as she kept up with them. Set into the walls were endless rows and towers of shelves and cabinets lined with artifacts whose nature she couldn't quite discern.… She tried to hear what the teachers were saying, trying to figure out why exactly they thought they should take Jax *deeper* into this nameless building instead of calling an ambulance.

Trying to figure out if she should be afraid.

So far the teachers were ignoring her. Jax hadn't trusted them—she wasn't forgetting that. She couldn't. On the other hand, they just didn't feel that sinister. The man on the subway had been sinister, but these people didn't have that vibe. And they had to care enough about Jax to be so serious and preoccupied. Didn't they?

She wondered if the way she *felt* about things was the truth of them, whether instincts could be trusted more than the reasons you might think of—the reasons why the instincts might be wrong.

Her eyes lit on objects peeking out of wall niches, looming down from high shelves—a series of porous rocks and minerals, one of which bore the curling, weathered label POMPEII; glass cases of fossils and bones; a fancy gold pocket watch with Roman numerals; what looked like parts of antique machines she couldn't identify, convoluted and graceful with spirals and tubes and wheels of discolored, dented brass; and a peeling, faded old painting of a smiling, proper-looking gentleman in a black bowler hat leaning on a walking stick in a leafy, sunlit garden. That picture looked genteel, until she noticed there was a long and hairy tail curling down onto the ground behind him.

They turned another corner. The gurney pushed through a set of heavy drapes, and she followed, silky tassels brushing over her forehead and eyes.

The room behind the velvet drapes was only slightly less dim and musty than the wood-paneled, winding hallways that had led them into it.

What made it different was its airiness, topped by a high, domed ceiling painted with what reminded her—though it was too far above to be seen exactly—of slides she'd seen of the Sistine Chapel. Far beneath the dome, through which a silvery light filtered, was a raised platform. The teachers trundled the gurney around to the side of the platform and lifted Jax on; then they bent over him, talking, and Cara couldn't understand them.

"What's *wrong* with him?" she asked urgently as soon as there was a small lull in the burble of conversation.

"Poison," said Mrs. Omotoso over her shoulder.

"*Poison*?" cried Cara, her voice shrill.

"Sit down, dear. I know it's difficult. Be patient. Your brother's in good hands."

"Poison?" repeated Cara. "But then—but you're not doctors! Are you? So shouldn't we—we should call 911!"

"No," said Mrs. Omotoso, and turned back to Jax again. "Believe me. Doctors and hospitals can't help him. It's not that kind of poison."

One of the other teachers was rolling over a cabinet on wheels, whose shallow trays clicked open. Around Jax, who was hidden from her behind the wall of people, it slowly got brighter, a dimmer switch being turned up.

She looked around for a chair, as instructed. She had to trust them, she guessed—because what was the alternative? She could call 911, but what if Mrs. Omotoso was telling the truth and the doctors really *couldn't* do anything for Jax? Plus, how would she tell the operator where she was? And if she did, how could they get in here? She had a feeling this part of the building wasn't exactly open to the public.

No: right now, she didn't have much of a choice. She didn't see any way to go except hoping against hope that they were trustworthy.

She sank into a chair with a plush seat, the lumps and points of its carved wooden back digging into her own. (She turned to inspect it: the protrusions were fins, it turned out—the chair's back formed of entwined, leaping porpoises or dolphins.) It wasn't too comfortable, and she sat on the very edge, blinking away tears. Jax had called her because he was afraid of these people, and now, for all she knew, she might be giving them the power of life or death over him.

She looked at the small crowd surrounding him on the dais and the light beaming down from the domed ceiling. Then the scene blurred and disappeared, tears standing on her bottom lids without spilling. She softly touched her ring.

And while she had her finger on it and was gazing tear-ily at the circle of teachers, it seemed to her that they had wings on their back—great, elegant, long-feathered white wings.

She took her finger off the ring, and the wings melted away.

She touched the ring again, her tears drying in her eyes. The wings came back.

Angel wings? That was what they looked like.

*Angel* wings? Come on. Seriously.

Mrs. M had a thing for angels, she thought, angels and Hummel figurines. Both tacky. Mrs. M's angels were mostly ceramic cherubs, fat and grinning and clutching arrows or trumpets in their pudgy fists....

But maybe she was being too literal. Maybe the flames hadn't really been in the subway guy's mouth and the wings weren't really on the teachers' backs, either. Maybe all the flames had meant was that the man was dangerous, that he had ravenous appetites and intended to do her harm. And maybe all the wings meant was the opposite: that despite Jax's suspicions, the teachers were trustworthy. That she should trust her instincts, as well as her visions, and the teachers were no threat to Jax.

She hoped.

Of course, there were plenty of other ways to interpret the appearance of wings. Such as, maybe they meant the teachers could travel fast, or they were going to go somewhere. The possible meanings were practically infinite.

"*Poison*," she said out loud to herself. If it was poison, and he'd been here the whole time, wouldn't these same people *have* to have been the ones to poison him?

And then she remembered the tacky souvenir pen.

*Ow!* Jax had said, grumpily. *That thing scratched me!*

Scratched him.

"Hey," she called out to Mrs. Omotoso's straight back, getting up from the chair. "So does—is there a guy named Roger who works here? A scientist from Woods Hole?"

Another of the teachers turned around, a balding man with a big bumpy nose that looked like it had been broken.

"Roger? No, there's no Roger on our staff," he said, and looked at her quizzically.

"But he *said* he was," said Cara. "He said he was a *consultant*. Then he gave me a pen to give to Jax, and left. I remember noticing because he didn't take the elevator, he took the stairs. And while Jax and I were sitting on the bunk bed, the pen scratched his leg."

Mrs. Omotoso turned around, and then another teacher, until most of the seven gathered there were looking at Cara. A short, frizzy-bearded teacher flipped open a cell and talked into it rapidly, his voice too low to hear. He wore thick glasses with black frames; he must have been the one she saw on Skype.

"And where did you meet this Roger?"

"Just at the elevator near Jax's room," said Cara. "When I got here." They must think she was such a dolt, taking what turned out to be a poison pen—who knew they really existed?—from a stranger. "I mean, I *know* him a little from before, he works—he used to work with my—with our mother. At Woods Hole, in marine biology."

The bearded, bespectacled teacher looked at another and nodded, then strode off through the door again, his cell held to one ear.

"It's very good that you told us, Cara," said Mrs. Omotoso quietly. "It's very good that we know."

Then she reached up and pulled a painted screen toward her, a screen on rollers that unfolded like an accordion, and Cara was shut out.

She got restless after a couple more minutes sitting in the knobby carved chair; she could hardly bear not knowing if Jax was going to be all right. She thought of calling someone, Max or Hayley or even Mrs. M or her dad, but she thought it dully and without momentum—as though it was preordained that she couldn't call anyone. Not until this part was over. Right now there was no way she could explain. So she got up and began a slow circuit of the room, walking along the wall, trying not to think about Jax's still, pale face.

Mrs. Omotoso had called it an infirmary, but it wasn't anything like the hospital room Max had been in when he broke his arm. For one thing, Cara didn't see medical equipment. There were books and yellowing maps, like in an antiquarian library; there were glass-topped tables at waist height, full of medieval-looking pages from old books with fancy, gilded letters in what appeared to be Latin. There were Asian scrolls with pagoda-style temples and watercolor trees on them, dragons and lions and bulgy-eyed fish. There were mosaics made of small tiles in brilliant colors; one looked like the sun, but the rays coming from it were snakes, and another was of a naked man with beard and trident, riding a chariot pulled by seahorses over some foaming ocean waves.

The artifacts seemed delicate and precious—and *old*. But maybe they were just fakes—they made great replicas these days, her mother had told her, of practically everything. There were copies of great paintings that most people couldn't tell from the real ones—some hanging in museums, to be admired by audiences who never knew the difference.

Did all the kids at the Institute come in here? Had Jax been in here before and already seen this? Maybe they studied this, maybe it was part of what they did…she'd thought they would be doing math and computers all the time. It hadn't occurred to her there would be history or art or subjects like that.

But now she'd come to a section that was hundreds of wooden cubbies stretching up to the ceiling, and in each hole stood a bottle or sometimes several of them. They were a great variety of shapes and sizes—large, handmade-type bottles shaped like bottom-heavy teardrops, tall green-tinted thin ones like pillars with old cork stoppers in the top, murky fluid inside and things floating in it.

Suddenly she caught sight of a bumpy white line inside one of them—a line up a minuscule back. It was a *spine*. She turned away, shocked, and walked fast past the rest of the bottles, concentrating on not looking.

Dead things in jars. That didn't exactly bode well.

If she thought of that and then the painting of the man with the tail—if she thought of the darkness in the corners....

Jax might be right about these people. Her own instincts might be dead, dead wrong. After all, Jax was the genius in the family. Not her.

Skirting a wooden ladder on wheels, she was close to the dais—close to the huddle of the teachers with their trays and lights, bent over Jax. There was a gap, she realized, a gap between the screen and the wall, near where the top of Jax's body should be; if she stood on one of the rungs of the ladder she might be able to see what they were doing.... She grabbed a rung and stepped up. One rung, then two, then three; her feet creaked when she put her weight on the wood. But she was three feet up now, and the backs of some of the teachers' heads were in her line of sight—the bald man, an elegant woman with sleek, bobbed silver hair.

She craned her neck to see between them. But the gaps were too narrow, after all. So she stepped up to the fourth rung.

And there was her brother, bathed in light.

There were streams and threads of light falling across his face and his bare chest (they'd taken off his shirt, which made him look even younger). The light fell over him in lines that crossed each other and made patterns. After a few moments she realized the narrow strings of light came from things the teachers were holding—handheld instruments that might have been pens or scalpels or even wands, for all she knew. She couldn't tell. Just small, thin sticks in their hands.

It was beautiful, how the light fell. Like spiderwebs or cat's cradles or graceful woven nets.

Could it be laser beams? Surgeons used lasers, after all. But these threads weren't sharp and straight; they were curved and soft. They were so lovely, in fact, that it was hard to believe they could be doing Jax any harm. It *had* to be a good light. It even felt good to her, some distance away. Its threads were soothing to look at: she watched in awe as they danced and trembled, joined and parted again.

The teachers were silent as they worked. She wondered what they had in common. Mrs. Omotoso looked African;

the bearded man who'd left before had caramel-colored skin, like maybe he was from the Middle East, she wasn't sure. Then there were white people—the bald man was white, the elegant woman with the silver hair…one other woman might be East Indian…what were they, those beautiful threads of light?

Then Mrs. Omotoso turned and caught her looking down at them. Feeling almost guilty, Cara was startled and looked away.

" 'Any sufficiently advanced technology is indistinguishable from magic,' " said the teacher.

"Pardon?"

"It's not my own. I'm just quoting—a famous line from the science-fiction writer Arthur C. Clarke. *Any sufficiently advanced technology is indistinguishable from magic.*"

"OK," said Cara uncertainly.

"That doesn't mean, of course, that magic isn't real."

⚎

"The poison wasn't the kind you find in bottles with skulls and crossbones on them," said the balding teacher with the broken nose. His name was Mr. Sabin, and he had a voice so deep it was almost comic. "It wasn't the kind they can pump out of your stomach or soak up with charcoal."

They sat at a thick oak table not far from where Jax was lying, apparently in a recovery mode, on his dais: Mr. Sabin, Mrs. Omotoso, and Cara. The other teachers had left the room when they finished with their light sabers (as Cara thought of them).

"It was for his mind. His mind that makes him so special," said Mrs. Omotoso.

She'd brewed a kettle of tea on a hot plate in the corner and sipped from a steaming cup of it now; Cara smelled lavender, a tea her mother also drank. Cara didn't like it, but she loved how it smelled. In their corner of the big, high-ceilinged room there were deep, overstuffed armchairs and a few floor lamps that shed a quiet orange light. Behind them were shelves of leatherbound volumes, and beneath their feet was an intricate rug that might have been Turkish. It reminded her of the flying carpets depicted in her old Arabian Nights treasury.

"Special," repeated Cara.

She felt dazed by what had happened; she wondered if she was all here.

How much did they know about Jax?

"Jax has a very special mind," said Mrs. Omotoso.

"But we don't have to tell *you* that," added Mr. Sabin. "You're his sister."

"Yeah. Jax is really smart," said Cara, and nodded carefully.

The two teachers glanced at each other sidelong.

"Smart, yes," said Mrs. Omotoso. "But that's not what we're talking about."

"It's not?" asked Cara.

She wondered if this was the moment where Jax's ESP

got them locked up. She saw, in a flash, both of them being kept as prisoners here, in the company of relics. Confined here along with the paintings of fine-looking gentlemen who were secretly devils, tails curving behind them. Along with the bottles of grisly, pickled specimens…

But at least, when she thought it, she wasn't touching the ring. Maybe it wasn't, in fact, a glimpse of the future.

"We know about Jax's talents," said Mrs. Omotoso. "At least, we know about some of them. You don't have to conceal your own knowledge, dear."

Cara didn't know what to say. Or whether she should speak at all.

"We think it's time we brought you in," said Mr. Sabin.

His voice was so deep it was a spoof of deep voices.

"Brought me in," she repeated warily.

"Now that you're involved, we think you need to know more than you do."

"There's a reason we've been keeping Jax here with us, you see," said Mrs. Omotoso.

"I thought he was here for—I thought it was an educational project?" faltered Cara.

"Of course, we *do* help bright students develop their talents," said Mr. Sabin. "But in Jax's case it was more of a pretext."

"Cara," said Mrs. Omotoso, and set down her china cup on its saucer delicately, "we brought your brother here to protect him. Because something is happening."

"You—you mean…"

She didn't know how much she could say. Would her *mother* want her to talk openly to these people? Jax hadn't trusted them. Jax's not trusting them was why she was here in the first place.

"We *know* Jax didn't trust us," said Mr. Sabin. "We know that's why he called you. Although, to be perfectly honest, we didn't find out about the call till afterwards. Jax concealed it. As we concealed our own minds from him."

Cara stared at him.

He could do it, too. Couldn't he.

"Excuse me," he said, nodding apologetically. "Yes. Jax has far more raw talent than I do, but I have experience on my side. As do all of the teachers here. I assure you, I usually ask permission to read people. We all ask permission. Unless we're dealing with hostiles. But this isn't a typical situation."

"We share some characteristics with your brother, you see, Cara," said Mrs. Omotoso.

She took the beaded headband out of her hair, flicked it onto her wrist absent-mindedly, and then smoothed her hair back and replaced the band more neatly. The familiarity of the gesture comforted Cara.

She had to rely on her intuition, she thought. It had gone OK so far, hadn't it? *Rely on your intuition.* Her mother had told her that.

"We call them 'the old ways.' Those senses your brother has. The thing about your brother is that he has more old-way abilities than—well, than most other people who have them," said Mrs. Omotoso. "He kind of has, or will have—well, it looks to us like he has…."

"Basically everything," said Mr. Sabin.

"What do you mean, *everything*?"

"Well," said Mrs. Omotoso, as she got up to lift the teapot off the hot plate and pour herself some more, "what he means is, most of us have one innate talent—one old way that we were born with and work to develop as we grow up. The old ways tend to run in families."

Mr. Sabin cleared his throat but didn't say anything.

"I'm what we call a mindtalker, for instance," went on Mrs. Omotoso, "and Mr. Sabin here is a mindreader, but Jax can do both of those things, can't he? And quite a number more."

"That makes him very valuable," said Mr. Sabin. "And unfortunately, very vulnerable, too."

"In this war," said Mrs. Omotoso, spooning honey into her cup, "he occupies a unique position. He's…well, people know about him. People on both sides. Do you remember that verse your mother left for you?"

"The poem about the *Whydah*? The shipwreck?"

"That was part of a longer—I guess you might call it a prophecy. And in the full prophecy, Jax is important. You are, too."

"Wait. My mother didn't write it? I thought she wrote it for us. As instructions that other people wouldn't get."

"No, dear. That text is far older than your mother."

"An old prophecy…that talks about Jax? And me?"

Mr. Sabin nodded gravely.

"And a couple of weeks ago something happened that made Jax...more exposed than he used to be," said Mrs. Omotoso. "So until we could get permanent protections into place—around your home and Jax's school—we brought him here."

"But as you saw, they reached him anyway," said Mr. Sabin, and cast a look over at the dais, where Jax appeared to be sleeping. "Luckily, I think we got to him in time to prevent permanent damage."

"*What* happened," said Cara. "*What* happened a couple of weeks ago?"

She wasn't giving them any information, she thought, but it didn't matter, because they knew it anyway. Even this, what she was thinking *right now*, was audible to Mr. Sabin. If he wanted it to be. She might as well be yelling her deepest secrets from a rooftop.

She felt deflated, as well as spied on. Before this, her brother was the only one who had been able to see into her mind. And that had been bad enough.

"I won't keep doing it," said Mr. Sabin. "I promise. As of right now, I'm not going to listen. I'll agree to trust you if you agree to trust me. OK?"

Cara hesitated a moment and then nodded reluctantly.

"Cara, we want you to brace yourself a little," said Mrs. Omotoso. "It's your mother."

She leaned in close and took Cara's hands.

Cara's anxiety spiked.

"She's not hurt," said Mr. Sabin quickly. "She has some excellent defenses. Believe me."

"But she is *captive*," said Mrs. Omotoso. "The enemy has her confined. And so she can't help you or your brother. Not right now."

So it turned out that if Cara hadn't been there, Roger wouldn't have been able to get to Jax at all.

In a way, it was her fault.

Or at the very least, her *and* Jax's fault, since he'd begged her to come. But poor Jax was the victim. She shouldn't have come, she thought, she shouldn't have listened to him; she shouldn't have broken the rules. She should have just called her dad. What had she been thinking? She should have done it all differently.

Roger couldn't have gotten near to Jax himself, because Jax would have read him, Mrs. Omotoso said, and then Jax could have run. Roger was a regular person, she said. He couldn't stop people like Jax or Mr. Sabin from reading his mind any more than Cara herself could. So, since Jax would read him the second he got near, he'd needed a go-between. Someone who wouldn't have any *idea* what was in his head and would carry the poison to Jax without even knowing they were doing it.

In other words, Cara.

"But how did Roger know I was going to be here, then? How *could* he know?"

"He must have intercepted Jax's communications with you, Cara. Did Jax send you an email?" asked Mr. Sabin.

"A text."

"Hmm."

"Wait. Roger read our *texts*?"

"Safe to assume he's been a spy for some time now," said Mr. Sabin. "Assigned to your mother. And she must not know that yet, or she would have reported him."

"But—I think my mother can mindtalk," said Cara. "Can't she? She communicated with me this summer without being near. Wouldn't she have known? Couldn't she have seen through him?"

"Your mother does have some mindtalk abilities, that's true," said Mrs. Omotoso. "She's above-average, definitely, talent-wise. But she's not a mind*reader*. On that score she's just intuitive, even if you sometimes feel she sees through you. In that way she's just a normal mother. So, no: she couldn't have read Roger, so she wouldn't automatically have known that he was working for the Cold."

"Him? It's *him*?"

"It's always him," said Mr. Sabin.

Suddenly he seemed very tired.

"So then—what is this place? If it's guarded against the elementals?"

"It's guarded against all the Cold One's methods, and it's one place of many," said Mrs. Omotoso. "I guess you could call it a sanctuary."

On the outside, the Institute didn't look out of the ordinary at all. It wasn't supposed to, she told Cara. But it had security. It was a fort constructed to keep out the people they didn't want to get in. That included all mindtalkers and mindreaders who weren't expressly invited, said Mrs. Omotoso. It was by invitation only.

"No shapeshifters, either," said Mr. Sabin. "Unless, of course, they're *our* shapeshifters."

Mrs. Omotoso shot him a look that seemed, to Cara, like a warning.

"I saw one this summer," said Cara. "We called him the Pouring Man. He was an elemental, my mother said, who worked for the bad guys? She said the elementals operate in one of four, like, Greek elements, water or earth or air or—"

"Fire," said Mr. Sabin.

"Anyway," she went on, "he was a water elemental, and he took the shape of my friend Hayley."

"Elementals aren't real shapeshifters," said Mr. Sabin. "They're not changing their shape—just your perception of that shape. *Real* shapeshifters rearrange their molecules. It's one of the highest-order talents."

"We don't want to burden her with *too* much right off the bat," said Mrs. Omotoso sharply.

Cara had the feeling, from her annoyed expression, that Mr. Sabin was breaking a private rule they'd agreed to.

"You told me what this place is," said Cara. "But, I mean—who are *you*?"

In the silence that followed, she could hear the slow ticking of an aged, analog clock on the wall.

"We're just people," said Mr. Sabin after a minute, "who are gifted in the old ways. And want to help others who are, too. We want to stop the Cold."

"But I know that's not the whole story," protested Cara. "I'm not *stupid*. Because the enemy has these—old ways, too! Don't they? Or some weird powers, anyway. So then what is it that *they* want? What are you *fighting* over? I wish you guys wouldn't keep speaking in code. My mother did that, too, the last time I saw her."

"There's a reason for it, Cara. I promise. We don't *want* to keep you in the dark, but we have to, partly. We need you to have enough information to help Jax and help your mother," said Mrs. Omotoso, "but not enough to put you in more danger than you already are."

"That's how it was before," said Cara.

She was frustrated, tired, and also thirsty, she realized. Her head ached dully. "Could I please have some water?"

"Of course," said Mr. Sabin, and got up, headed for the corner cabinet that held the lavender tea.

"That's because this war is *all about information*," said Mrs. Omotoso. "It's about what people know and what they don't want to know. We have to be very cautious when it comes to knowledge. Because knowledge is not simply power. It's the bridge between beings; in some sense it's the *medium* of being. We have an old saying: 'Knowledge is the language that exists outside time.'"

Cara didn't quite follow that and didn't have the energy to try.

"What kind of information?" she persisted.

Her throat was so parched it felt like it was going to crack, so she was immensely grateful when Mr. Sabin handed her a glass of water. It was a goblet, in fact, an old cut-crystal one, and heavy in her hand as she tipped it up and drained it. The water wasn't cold, but it did taste clean.

"Information about what's happening to the world and why," said Mrs. Omotoso gravely. "Information not only about the history of civilization, but about its future."

Cara gazed around her, letting the water sink into her dry throat. She let her head fall back so that she could see the paintings on the domed ceiling through particles of dust that were drifting lazily in the light. There were high windows beneath the dome, but that didn't quite explain the way light filtered through…. Now that she had some time to study the dome, she saw it wasn't much like the Sistine Chapel after all. At least, not like the only part of the Sistine Chapel she remembered from art class, which was two naked men with fingers touching. (Or maybe one of them wasn't naked; possibly God had worn a pink robe….) Anyway, it wasn't like that, really; it was more of a scene of animals, all kinds of animals in a garden.

"Jax said he found a source," she said finally, when her throat felt better. "In my mother's research. Of carbon gases going into the ocean? He said he thought knowing about it was putting him in danger. Except—well, he thought the danger was from you guys. But is that why Roger poisoned him?"

"Part of it," nodded Mrs. Omotoso. "What your mother and then Jax discovered is definitely something the enemy wants to keep hidden. We know *what* it is; we just didn't know exactly where. Your mother found out *where*."

"Is she—is she going to be OK? I mean—if she's a prisoner, what will they do to her?"

Mrs. Omotoso and Mr. Sabin exchanged glances again.

"Your mother is a kind of hostage," said Mr. Sabin finally. "That's what we believe."

"A hostage?" asked Cara. "But then—are there demands, or whatever? Isn't that what they do with hostages?"

"We know what they want," said Mrs. Omotoso. "They're holding her to stop her protecting someone else. Someone they haven't been able to take directly yet but did manage to hurt; someone whose potential command of knowledge makes him into a weapon. They tried to bring him over once this summer, and now they're trying again."

"We're fairly sure," said Mr. Sabin, "that more than your mother, Jax is the one they really want."

❦

She woke up and thought two things: first, she'd forgotten about the swim meet, forgotten about her phone, forgotten Hayley and Mrs. M and her responsibilities and regular life.

Second, she must have passed out.

She wasn't the type to do that; she'd never fainted in her life, but then they'd said something about the bad guys

70

wanting her little brother, and then a slow slide and…nothing. And now here she was.

*Here* was a dim, quiet room, in one of two twin beds with fringed canopies hanging over them; a few feet away, in the other bed, was someone else. She raised herself on her elbows to look. Jax.

The pale-green coverlet over him rose and fell minutely; he seemed to be sleeping. She fell back and then propped herself up, plumping the pillows behind her head. Clearly she was still in the old part of the building, because the walls were covered with paintings hanging close together in golden, scalloped frames. There was no way this was part of the modern shell that housed the outer, more public rooms of the Institute.

It was almost, she realized, as if the building she'd seen from the street—the gray, boxlike office building with the large, square numbers of its street address—had been built around an ancient hub, as if that building with the gleaming, fluorescent lobby was a kind of bright new armor for an older heart. It seemed to her that this inner sanctum might have been here for hundreds of years, slowly amassing its libraries of worn books, its trove of treasures and sometimes (inside the jars she hadn't wanted to look at) of horrors, too.

The paintings that covered the wall beside her bed were all portraits, she saw—portraits from different periods, it looked like. Some were more cracked and chipped than others; some were so muddy she could hardly make out what they depicted; some had glass over them and others did not. Some were very flat looking, and it was because, she realized, they didn't even use perspective, which she remembered was an advance that painters made at a certain point in history. The portraits were mostly of people, mostly in fancy clothes and formally posed; most of them looked smug or imperious or arrogant or, at the very least, puffy.

On a table beside her bed there were miniatures, paintings in oval settings not larger than the palm of her hand. She rolled over and gazed at them—noblemen and noble-women, maybe, like the ones on the walls. But there was also something stranger: portraits of animals. One of them looked a little like an anteater, except that it had brown scales; one looked like a big duck; one looked like an ocean-going creature, with a long, slender neck and flippers.

Very bizarre, she thought lazily.

She was still wearing her same clothes, she registered in relief as she woke up more, but there were no windows in this room, so she had no idea what time it was.

Peering over the side of the bed she found her pack on the lower level of the bedside table; she grabbed it by a strap and pulled her phone from the outside pocket.

It read 6:14.

And also You Have 7 New Text Messages.

She jumped out of the bed. Both her feet hit the rug at the same time, bedclothes partly snarled around her legs.

And then she realized there wasn't much she could do. *It was six o'clock.*

When it came to Mrs. M, she was screwed.

She sat down heavily on the edge of the bed, untwisting the trailing coverlet from her ankle, and brought up the list of texts. They were all from Hayley.

The first read *Come bak ASAYGT, shes asking abt u. Sed u wr sik in BR.*

Then *WAYN? Tell me! Come bak!*

Then *OMG. Weer n dp sht.*

Then *Call me ASAP.*

Then *Goin bak 2 hotel. Had 2 tell hr re Jax.*

Then *She wants 2 cal yr dad.*

Then *She wants 2 cal the cops.*

Cara squeezed her eyes shut and took a deep breath. Then she started punching the numbers in to call her dad at home, and was lifting the phone to her ear when there was a knock on her room door.

It was Mrs. O.

Cara pushed the hangup button, holding off.

"I think you needed that rest," said the teacher. "You were exhausted."

"But—my friend's mom wants to call the police!" burst out Cara. "Mrs. Moore, who I told you about? Who's in charge of me on the trip? I got a text about it. I'm going to be in *such* trouble!"

Mrs. O shook her head.

"I spoke with her," she said. "The number was right there on your cell, so I took the liberty. I told her you and Jax were here. I said you were both under our care, that Jax had gotten upset and asked you to come get him. I said you were spending the night here and we'd drop you off tomorrow."

Cara exhaled, then turned back to look at her brother.

"*Is* he better?" she asked, and tiptoed to the side of his bed to bend over the sleeping form. She could see his eyes making small, trembling movements beneath the shadowed eyelids. "Is he *really*?"

"His physical health is fine," said Mrs. O. "We won't know about the rest until he wakes. We did what we could. And my guess is, he'll be in this deep sleep for a while yet."

"What should I do about—I mean, I'm supposed to be with the swim team. I'm supposed to do a relay tomorrow. In the morning."

"Come, have dinner with the rest of us," said Mrs. O, and beckoned. "You need to eat a square meal."

"But—and just leave Jax here? Alone? What if he wakes up alone?"

"He needs his rest," said Mrs. O. "And security's on high alert now anyway; this room is protected, though I know you can't see that. The light treatment we gave your brother has…draining side effects."

Cara saw there was a pedestal sink in the corner, towels neatly hanging on a brass rack beside it, and walked over to scoop cold water onto her face and neck.

"Did they catch Roger, then?" she asked when she had dried off again. She felt better already.

"Not yet," said Mrs. O.

Cara took a last look at Jax as she followed the teacher out the door: he seemed peaceful in the dim light, surrounded by the walls of portraits—as though they were looking down on him, a host of guardians.

*Four*

*Cara went to supper at a long table in the Institute's kitchen,* a room that was so big she couldn't see all of it at once. It was down several flights of stairs from the room under the high dome—in the core of the building, as Mrs. O called it.

There was the "core" and the "shell," she'd told Cara as they came in; the core was the old part and the shell was the new, which looked like a thousand other office buildings. Like the rest of the rooms in the core, the kitchen had no windows, but there were open fireplaces at each end. And there was an actual stone floor with big gray flagstones, which made her wonder how many floors there could be beneath it. After all, a stone floor had to be heavy.

The table was lined with adults she assumed were teachers. She sat down beside Mrs. O, and someone handed her a plate with spaghetti and sauce on it, then a small bowl full of grated cheese with a delicate silver spoon. Cara was reaching for the spoon, idly wondering why the parmesan wasn't just in a green-plastic shake container like it should be, when it occurred to her that half the teachers could be reading her mind at that very instant.

Her hand went a little limp.

"So—if some of the people here are mindreaders," she said under her breath to Mrs. O, "does that mean they're reading me right now? Because with Jax…"

"No, dear, we have an amnesty," said Mrs. O, smiling. "What Mr. Sabin was talking about. Amnesty's what we call it between friends. We don't use the old ways on each other unless there's either a clear crisis or a personal understanding. That's why we didn't find out about Roger until you told us. We don't read people as a matter of course—only when we feel we have no other choice."

"In that case," said the bearded teacher with the glasses, "we erred on the other side, didn't we? Big mistake. We were so busy with Jax, we didn't bother to read you. Or we might even have caught up to Roger."

"In other words, don't worry," said the teacher with the neatly cut silver hair. "You'll have the usual amount of privacy while you're eating your spaghetti."

"Unless you do something that enrages us, that is," said the bearded teacher, jokey. "By the way, I'm Glen. Or Mr. Trujillo, if you prefer. Like the despot."

Cara went to reach for the spoon again, but the bowl of parmesan had already moved down the table. Still, she was too hungry to wait, so she started to eat without it.

"I didn't get to tell Jax this," she said slowly, twirling spaghetti on her fork as Mrs. O poured herself a glass of red wine from a fat-bottomed bottle in the middle of the table and Mr. Trujillo, across from them, forked up salad in a messy way that left white dabs of dressing on his beard.

"But I have a question about something I saw? In a—I guess it was a vision?"

"Go on," said Mrs. O.

"Spill it," said Mr. Trujillo.

"So the vision was—well, I saw this *man* in a subway train, and it seemed to me he was following me. We were alone in the subway car. I have this ring my mother gave me, and when I looked at him and touched the ring, he opened his mouth..."

The teachers were both waiting, gazing at her.

"...and it looked like there were these *flames* in there."

Mr. Trujillo let his fork hand rest on the edge of the table, the lettuce sticking out and trembling a bit.

Mrs. O put her wine down and swallowed.

"A vision of a Burner," she said quietly.

Mr. Trujillo raised his napkin with his free hand and patted at his beard.

"A *Burner*?" asked Cara.

"They used to be called fire-eaters," said Mr. Trujillo, nodding. "They were made by the Cold, some time ago. They're part of his army. He was in England first, you know. That is, his army operated there. Birmingham, England, in the 1740s. Paul and Wyatt—"

"Birmingham?" echoed Cara.

She had no idea what he was talking about.

"It was all his work, you see...he was behind it all. The first mills, the first seeds of what would be a world-wide movement toward the massive use of coal. The poet William Blake wrote about it. Those *dark Satanic mills*...."

"You're being obscure, Glen," said Mrs. O. "As usual. She won't know anything about that. They probably haven't even gotten to the Industrial Revolution in her history class yet. Nor is she *ready*, Glen, for our...particular take on it."

"Later, in the 1850s," went on Mr. Trujillo, holding his napkin out in front of him and apparently studying the food smears upon it, "they were also linked to some people in the South who were extremists in support of slaveholding for tobacco and cotton. Who helped get the Civil War started, in fact. Although that was only a side project, basically a hobby, for the most part—"

"Glen's point is, they've been around for a long time," interrupted Mrs. O brusquely. "And that's only possible because they're not, in fact, human."

"They're like the Pouring Man, then?" said Cara. "Elementals?"

"Yes," said Mrs. O. "That's exactly right. The Burners are fire elementals."

"I thought I might have—that it might just have been one of these visions that I get," said Cara. "Like when I saw wings on you. But they weren't really physical wings. Were they?"

In the corner of the kitchen, someone clanged a pot, and it rang out in the stillness.

"Sorry to disappoint. The Burners' flames are real," said Mr. Trujillo.

The other teachers were definitely listening now. Most had even stopped eating, though some still lifted their wine glasses and sipped. It made her a bit nervous.

"The humanoid forms they take are just camouflage. They need a certain amount of heat to manifest, and they also give it off," went on Mr. Trujillo. "In a pinch they can use flammables instead of an open flame—the gas in the tanks of cars, for instance, or lighters or some kinds of alcohol…."

"They carry whole microclimates with them," said Mrs. O. "So usually you feel them before you see them."

Cara remembered the heat of the subway car. At the time she'd thought it must be what always happened, that when the train stopped maybe the air-conditioning shut down… But wait: If the Burner *had* been real, what did he want with *her*?

Another teacher spoke sharply from the end of the table—the East Indian woman. She had her hair braided up on her head and a dark red spot between her eyebrows.

"My dear, listen closely: this is important. Where did you have this vision? And *when*?"

"On the T," said Cara. "On my way here."

Then suddenly all the teachers were talking among themselves—or no: they were *thinking* at each other. It made her catch her breath: ripples like waves in the air, like the shimmer above a road in the desert heat. They were identical to the ones she'd seen flow between Jax and the leatherback sea turtle in the Aquarium back in August.

All around her the air was moving, somehow—like a turbulence, a minor half-visible storm, twisting ribbons that distorted the view like a warped mirror or the patterned plastic of a shower door.

She gazed up into it, amazed. Technically the silence around the table was wearing on, but at the same time the air was bristling with energy she could almost hear—a kind of liquid back-and-forth of pulses and lulls, so that the silence seemed less like the absence of sound and more like some kind of low-level white noise. It felt almost like the ocean, with currents and rhythm and deep pulls below....

But it didn't last. After what couldn't have been more than a few seconds, all of the teachers were standing. They seemed to be deserting their meals and their half-full, richly red glasses of wine. Some of them almost seemed to glide away, Cara thought, and remembered the wings.

She felt at a loss until Mrs. O's hand on her arm guided her up from the table, up and—with the crowd in front of them and behind them, too—out the door they'd come in through.

"Was it what *I* said?" asked Cara, though it was half whisper and half thought.

*Partly,* thought Mrs. O into Cara's head.

Her thought had the high, pure sound Jax's had had—as though, in the space of Cara's brain, completely different people's voices got translated into the same kind of music. And yet, she knew it was Mrs. O. The idea "coincidence" came to her more as a feeling than as a word, a feeling or maybe a minor vision: in this case, a small mental picture of two parallel lines, which she instinctively knew meant *coincidence*.

*We sensed their presence then*, sang the mind of Mrs. O into Cara's. It sounded like a tuning fork, that resonating tone. She'd heard a tuning fork in music class one time last year. Not exactly relaxing. When the thoughts came from Jax ,it wasn't as jarring.

"Sensed it?" asked Cara.

*They're coming.*

"But I thought this was a *sanctuary*, where the bad guys couldn't get in," protested Cara.

"It is," said Mrs. O out loud. "But all fortresses can be breached. The enemy is focusing a lot of energy, as we speak, on breaking down our wards—our defenses. And sooner or later they'll succeed."

⚎

With Mrs. O and Mr. Trujillo alongside, Cara raced up stairways and through corridors to the bedroom where Jax lay sleeping—only now, when they pushed the door open, he was awake.

He was sitting on the edge of his canopy bed.

"Jax!" said Cara, and ran up to him.

He stayed slumped over, head bowed.

"Jax?" she asked, sitting down on the edge of the mattress beside him. "Jax? Are you OK?"

83

Still he didn't say anything; slowly he raised his head and turned to look at her.

His *eyes*, she thought. They'd changed again. Now the pupils were huge; the pupils were the whole iris. The blue of his eyes was completely gone. The irises were black—and not sharply black but a black that faded around the edges, fuzzed into the white of the eyes.

"What's *wrong* with him?" she asked urgently, turning to the teachers. "Why are his *eyes* like that?"

They were at the bedside now, too, on the other side from Cara, their hands passing over Jax's head in a strange fashion.

"Because the treatment failed," said Mr. Trujillo.

He shook his head, glancing grimly at Mrs. O.

"We're going to have to take him with us," said Mrs. O, more to him than to Cara.

Although her hands were moving over Jax, they weren't, Cara noticed, quite touching him. Jax wasn't saying anything; she couldn't imagine him speaking, the way he was now. He just stared at them emptily.

"What do you mean, take him?" asked Cara.

"When we go," said Mrs. O.

"We're going to have to go," agreed Mr. T. "The wards are still up now, but they're breaking down fairly quickly. I can feel it happening. We can rebuild them, but not fast enough."

"But—go where?"

"We're leaving—though not through the front door," said Mrs. O. Her hands fluttered, seeming to draw Jax's face

84

forward, and then fell. "We have to abandon this place for a while."

"You have to leave, too. But you won't be coming with us," added Mr. T. "We need you to do something else. Something crucial."

"But I can't leave with Jax...like that!" said Cara. She felt on the brink of tears.

"You need to do this for him—do this so we can help him," he went on. "He's who they're here for. They were led to him."

"You mean by—by *me*?"

"Not your fault, Cara. Not at all," said Mrs. O quickly. "Anyone who loved him would have done the same. But he needs to be moved. Your mother's out there as their hostage, and she has something he needs if he's going to recover."

"We'll need something from her to bring him back," added Mr. T. "We have to stay out of sight and take care of him, so you're going to have to go get her. Either her or what we need from her. Whichever's possible. "

"And what do you need from her?"

"A memory."

"A *memory*? But how can I—"

"The memory of his birth," said Mr. T.

"Jax is *adopted*," said Cara.

"Yes, of course," said Mrs. O. "The memory of when she first saw him. Her earliest memory of him. She'll know, when you tell her what's happened. If you can find her, she should know how to help."

"But how am I supposed to do *that*? I haven't seen her for two months!"

"You have to use your own old way," said Mrs. O. "Work on your vision. It's your talent, Cara. You need to call it up."

"I don't know how!"

"We'd guide you, but there's no time. There's a book in the library here that should help," said Mr. T. "Look for the title…let's see, how did it go…yes: *Learning to See*. If I recall. It has an inscription on it, "Videre licet." That's on the cover, too, I think. *Videre licet*. Be listed in the card catalog."

As he said all this they were guiding Jax to his feet, standing him up between them. His arms hung limply; he gazed ahead, zombie-like.

"We have to take him now," said Mrs. O. "Can you feel it, Cara?"

The air in the room had gotten warmer. Cara touched her upper lip and felt a bead of perspiration.

She followed the two teachers out the door, walking behind them as they hustled Jax along the hall and rounded a corner.

"You'll need the code for the elevator," said Mr. T, and stopped walking to turn to her. "It's easy. Key in your own eight-digit birthdate, month first. You're in the system already. When you have what you need, come find us again."

"Jax is depending on you," said Mrs. O. "You can do this. But be careful. And be quick. You're safe here until the wards fail. But you don't want to be here when that happens."

"Jax? Hey. Jax?" asked Cara, leaning in to him.

She couldn't let go of the conviction that he was in there somewhere, and since he was in there, he *had* to respond to her...didn't he? And then, if she could just make him act like himself again, they wouldn't have to separate. She wouldn't be left alone, wouldn't have to do something hard that she had no clue about.

But he wasn't even turning to look at her as she spoke; all she could see was the back of his head. "Jax. Come *on*, Jax. It's me!"

She grabbed his arm and tried to turn him. The arm was rubbery, and his jaw, when she rotated him to face her, was still slack. And in his staring, impersonal eyes, their pupils huge and black, she saw what looked like an infinite void.

It was as though the pupils were so deep they went down forever, as black and silent as the vacuum of space.

It chilled her.

"Remember: *Crede quod habes, et habes,*" said Mr. T. "Latin."

Cara opened her mouth to tell him they didn't offer Latin at her school; so could he please speak English? But before she could get it together to speak, the boy who had been Jax, along with both of the teachers, melted into the wall.

❈

She was standing there awestruck, with an afterimage stamped on her mind of the three of them disappearing, when she realized she didn't have time to wonder how they'd done it. She didn't have time to think about what was going on with the other kids, in the shell of the building, or the rest of the teachers, or where exactly the Burners were.

Instead she shook off her questions and headed down through the maze of deserted corridors to the library to find the book.

It was spooky to be in there alone. Though the dome itself contained no glass, and of course there were no windows, an odd kind of light still shone down whitely from up high, as though leaking through invisible seams in the walls. It wasn't daytime anymore, but still the light beamed down with no clear source, dust motes whirling. As she made her way through the room, she was conscious of the jars in the cubbyholes, the bones in the display cases.

Was it getting hotter, she wondered? The back of her neck was clammy underneath the hair; strands stuck to the skin and made her itch.

How fast would the Burners get in?

Or would they possibly give up, if they sensed Jax had been moved away? Might they sense his absence and not be interested in coming in anymore? The Pouring Man had *sensed* where she and Jax were, after all. Max, too. He had found out where they were going and what they were doing, it seemed, more than once. He had known seemingly impossible things.

So maybe the fire elementals could do that, too. And maybe, hopefully, she wasn't a big enough prize for them…

but she still had to hurry. She had to figure out where to go and how to get there, and the book was her only hope.

In the wing of the great room that was devoted to bookshelves, where armchairs stood with floor lamps beside them on the fraying rugs, there was a wooden cabinet she thought must hold the card catalog. She hurried over and pulled out one of the trays. But there was nothing under "Learning to See" in the L's. (The nearby titles were curious: *Lean on Me: Brief Biographies of Famous Trees. Learning to Cope With H. Sapiens in 10 (Moderately) Easy Steps. Learning to Sing With Cetaceans: The Gift of Harmony.* But no *Learning to See.*)

She opened one drawer after another hastily until she found the Vs: how did you spell it? She tried *Vee—* first, then *Ve—*. Nothing. Then *Vi—*. It seemed to be by subject as well as by title or author, all combined in the one cabinet. Violets, Shrinking. Violence, Electrical…

*Videre licet.* Could that be it? The subtitle was "Learning to See." Had Mr. T gotten it the wrong way around? There was no author's name and only a simple number; it didn't look like the Dewey Decimal. Nor was the card attached to the drawer; she could pull it right out. So she did.

It must be late by now, she realized. She didn't wear a watch, and she hadn't looked at her cell recently, which was back in her backpack in the room she'd been sharing with Jax….

Jax of the dark eyes. The eyes like the vacuum of space.

The floor lamps had to be motion sensitive, she thought, like the light outside the garage at home, because as she moved toward them they flicked on. She counted the numbers on the shelves, consulting her index card as she moved quickly along; soon she was at a tall shelf of oversize books. Some of them were two or three feet tall, it looked like; some had to lie horizontally, they were so large.

She bent down to study their dusty spines and finally made out LEARNING TO SEE. A GUIDE. *Videre licet.*

She put down the card and reached for the book, which was beneath a pile of others, drawing it out carefully. It was a very large book—more than half as tall as she was, and quite a bit wider—but there wasn't enough light to read by so she carried it over to the oak table where she'd sat before with the teachers. A long reading light with a green glass shade flicked on as she placed the book flat on the table's surface and pulled out a chair.

Gingerly, because the book looked worn, she opened the book, thumb and index finger carefully holding the front cover. There was no jacket, only a faded blue cloth binding. As the cover rose, she saw it was covered in tiny eyes—tiny, faint images of eyes: there had to be thousands of them. And it must have a 3D effect sewn into the threads, she thought, because as the cover opened, the eyes seemed to open with it.

*Any sufficiently advanced technology*—she recalled Mrs. O saying to her in this same room—*is indistinguishable from magic.*

The first page was blank. That wasn't unusual. But then the next page was blank, too. And the next.

Maybe she needed a stronger light, she thought; maybe the type was faded. She pushed the book closer to the green light; it seemed to her that the light brightened further.

Still she couldn't see anything on the massive pages. They looked white as a field of fresh snow.

She turned a few pages further, slowly and deliberately, and then flipped to the back of the book, just in case.

Nothing.

She sat back in the chair, discouraged. Then panicky. Her time had to be running out. And what could she do, without the book? How would she ever find out where her mother was being kept?

She touched her ring quickly, still looking at the book.

But the pages stayed blank.

She raised her eyes from the empty pages and caught sight of a painting on the wall. It was a portrait of two young ladies from olden times; they had wide ruffed collars on, those giant white lacy things you saw on the first Queen Elizabeth. They always reminded Cara of the plastic cones vets put on dogs. Worrying the ring with her fingers, she wondered what she was supposed to do next. What would happen to Jax if she failed?

They hadn't told her that. They hadn't said what would happen to him. But it couldn't be good.

How could she figure out the book?

She wasn't really *looking* at the painting, she realized, though she was resting her eyes on it. It was lit by a small brass light above it, the kind they had at museums, which jutted out from the wall…and then, with a shock, she knew exactly what she was seeing.

The ladies had faces she knew, faces she recognized.

One of the ladies was Jaye.

And the other was Hayley.

Back in the bedroom with the twin beds, where she'd run till she was out of breath, she dug into her pack and pulled out her phone. Sure enough, there were more texts from Hayley; she didn't stop to read them. She dialed.

"Finally," groaned Hayley, picking up after one ring. "What's *up* with you?"

"So this is going to seem hard. But it's really important, Hay. I need you."

"*What*?"

"I need you to come to where I am—like now, right now. I need your help. I'll text you directions."

"Are you *kidding*? You know how my mom is. She'd wig if I asked to go out into the city after dark."

Part of her wanted to run to them instead, just take the book and go to the hotel herself, away from this place with its failing defenses. But so far the book wasn't helpful—what if it was the wrong one? If it turned out to be the wrong book entirely, she'd definitely need to be here to find the right one. She knew her friends could help.

"Please, Hay. *Please* come. And Jaye—I need her, too. I need both of you. I really do. I'll owe you big-time, I know I will. But this is for Jax. He's really sick. He got…he got poisoned."

"*Poisoned*?"

"I promise, this is way bigger than the meet."

"You *know* what would happen if Mom found out I snuck out. I'd be grounded till freshman year in *college*. If she even let me *go*, at that point."

Cara gazed at the miniature portraits beside the bed as she listened to Hayley protest. They were amazing in the fineness of their details, she thought…and she touched her ring again to see if these pictures, too, would turn into her friends. Nothing happened. It must have to do with thinking about something, she thought, as she made contact with the ring…some kind of focus she had to have, maybe? Not just a subject she had to be thinking of, but also a problem?

When she hung up, she still didn't know whether her friends would show up.

Or whether the Burners would get here first.

❈

Jax's room, she thought, for Jax's computer: that was where she had to go. If she couldn't figure out the book with the blank pages, maybe there would be a clue to finding her mother on there. She wasn't a computer whiz, but she knew more about laptops than about mysterious, blank books.

She found the part of the wall she thought she remembered was the elevator—the right angle where one of the narrow corridors turned a corner—but she didn't see any keypad. She wasn't sure she had the right place until she noticed that the light-switch plate didn't seem to fit neatly on the space behind it: there was a narrow vertical gap.

She reached out and touched it, and the plate slid to one side, exposing a modern-looking grid of numbered buttons. It took a couple of tries to get the digits of her birthdate entered; she flubbed a number once and had to start again. But on the next try the door slid open. It was perfectly silent: it didn't ding like a regular elevator.

She got in and stared at the console for a while. What floor was this? How would she get back? She looked up above the door to the strip of numbers. It read: 1, 1Ψ, 2, 2Ψ, 3, 3Ψ…she was on 8Ψ, it looked like. And Jax's room had been 822. So she hit the regular eight, and the door closed noiselessly and a split second later was sliding open again.

The fluorescents running along the ceiling shocked her eyes; she'd gotten used to the dim core, the dull gleam of low-wattage floor lamps and the torch-like sconces on the walls. The walls in the shell were bright and bland, the carpet—under the fluorescent lights—a strangely metallic gray that made her head throb dully behind the eyes. She felt like she'd suddenly been transported from ancient Greece to Walmart.

And it was definitely cooler out here.

The rest of the kids must have been moved, she thought, heading down the hall through the silence that seemed to buzz faintly. Maybe the elementals were dangerous to them, too. But the lights were still on, blazing for no one. A couple of room doors stood ajar, and through them she could see windows, once again—windows into the dark city with its spots of light that were also windows, the windows of other tall and unknown buildings.

Suddenly she felt more alone than she ever had. What if they didn't come? What would she do here, by herself?

Night had fallen.

Jax's room was more or less as they'd left it when they hustled him out, the covers on the bottom bunk still imprinted with two rounded dents where he and Cara had sat. The poisonous pen was gone, of course—the teachers must have taken it—but Jax's closed laptop sat on one of the desks, a tiny light on its side fading and brightening again.

She sat down and opened it; the screen lit up and prompted her for a password, which luckily she knew. Jax wasn't secretive the way Max was; he'd keyed in his password in front of her. Once she entered the word and its suffix of numbers, his email inbox popped up. She scrolled down, wishing she knew what she was looking for. Would he have bothered to hide what he found?

She saw emails from her, emails from Max—the normalcy of it was comforting, all Jax's everyday, kid emails.

Finally there was a raft of messages from his geeky best friend, Kubler. She felt guilty clicking on the first one; like she was spying, until the thought of Jax's black eyes firmed up her resolve.

There it was: a mention of the source. Kubler's reply didn't say much except *No way, that's so incredibly weird*, but Jax's email to him, below, read *I pinpointed the coordinates. It's along the Mid-Atlantic Ridge. Somewhere between Greenland and Norway. The volume is massive! Black smokers, is what it looks like. But what Mom's saying is*, these *black smokers aren't your typical geological features. These* are not natural.

Black smokers? It *had* to be her vision. Her vision *had* been of the source. And Jax hadn't kept all this a total secret: Kubler knew. That meant maybe someone had intercepted *these* messages, as well as Jax's texts to her. The bad guys— Roger or maybe even the elementals.

She thought back to the vision she'd had in her bedroom: dark, billowing smoke. And the scene beneath the smoke—snatches of light, apparently under the ocean floor. It seemed impossible, light under the ocean floor. Unless there was a subterranean volcano, maybe? She knew they existed, volcanoes beneath the sea. Could what she had seen be lava?

But Jax had written: "These are not natural." Quickly she googled "black smoker" and read *black smokers, or sea vents, are hydrothermal vents occurring on the ocean floor. They resemble dark chimney-like structures....*

So normally black smokers *were* natural. But these, according to Jax, were not. Did that mean the vents on the ocean floor were manmade? Made by the Cold?

Then, from her pack, her phone made a text alert sound. She fished it out and looked. It was from Jaye.

*We're here*, it said. *So come get us.*

In the lobby downstairs there was no one at the reception desk. The lights were on and the phone console at the desk was blinking; beside it lay a half-eaten sandwich with a piece of baloney sticking out. The night guard must have taken a bathroom break. Cara looked around warily, half expecting to see frightening men with flames leaping in their mouths.

But all she saw was Hayley and Jaye, standing near the revolving doors and looking a little stunned.

"No way were we getting on the T. We took a cab," said Hayley. "I had to sneak the money from my mom's purse. So you better pay me back. I'm in serious, serious crap already because of this. OK?"

"OK," said Cara gratefully. "Come on."

Hayley kept talking as they followed her to the elevators.

"You're lucky, by the way," she said. "That Zee totally took the heat off you. She did a disappearing act herself! Only there wasn't anyone covering for her."

"Really? Zee?"

Cara was puzzled. It didn't seem like Zee.

"Please. She was clearly pining for Max, after one night away," scoffed Hayley as Cara punched the button and the doors closed in front of them. "I bet they're shacked up in a sketchy motel as we speak. Catching some bedbugs to take home."

"Anyway," said Jaye softly (Cara thought she was trying to blunt Hayley's meanness). "It was kind of a coincidence. Two people going off campus at the same time. But then, with Zee being older, and I guess she doesn't have a stellar attendance record anyway, they're not as worried about her. Plus, Mrs. M wasn't in charge of Zee, or she'd have *really* freaked."

The number eight lit up, and the doors dinged open.

"This is the smart-kid think tank?" asked Hayley. "It doesn't look like much."

"Oh, it gets weirder," said Cara. "Don't worry."

She led them down the bright empty halls to the other elevator, the hidden one. There was a keypad here too, beneath a switch plate again; again she slid it open and keyed in her birthday.

"Cool," said Hayley when the wall opened noiselessly.

They stepped in, and before they were even settled the door reopened. They were inside the core.

"*Way* different," said Jaye as they walked through the narrow hall. On the walls the sconces glowed dimly.

"It's *hot* in here," said Hayley irritably.

"It *is* hot," agreed Jaye. "So is this—does this place have something to do with—"

"I *had* to tell her," interrupted Hayley, turning to Cara guiltily. "Otherwise she wouldn't have come with me!"

"You told her—" started Cara.

"I told her about August," said Hayley. "The pouring dude. How he reached out from the mirror. And the other Cara and Jax when we were in the boat. The shapeshifting or whatever. All the bizarro stuff that happened."

"I still think you're pulling my leg," said Jaye. "And if this turns out to be a prank, I'm going to be really hurt that you guys were playing with me."

Before Cara could answer, they were at the door to the huge room beneath the dome.

"Wow," breathed Hayley. "This place is wild."

"What *is* it?" asked Jaye as they stood on the threshold.

The heavy curtains were held back now and they could see the dome and the two wings of the room reaching out to the sides—the one with all the artifacts, on the left, and the one with all the books, on the right. There were some dim lights among the chairs and tables, but overall it was shadowy. The crannies and alcoves that were nestled into the dusty walls receded into darkness.

"You know what this reminds me of?" asked Jaye. "It's like the cathedrals my family went to in France last spring break. On that vacation where I decided I wanted to be an architect? If you look at those cathedrals from above, they have the shape of a cross. Like this room! That dome is what they call an apse, those two wings are the transept, and the big open part there is the nave. I really loved those old churches. I swear. This room is just like a church."

Cara looked around the room. Now that Jaye mentioned it, she thought her friend must be right. The raised platform where Jax had lain would be where the altar was.

Only this church was deeply imbedded in an office building.

"It didn't occur to me," she said, nodding slowly.

"But I don't understand," went on Jaye. "When I say *old*…I mean, you don't see places like this in the U.S. At all. It's basically medieval. Gothic, I think."

"There's a bunch of other stuff I could show you," said Cara. "But we need to get going. There's a task I have, to help Jax. Come on."

She led them to the library wing, one half of what Jaye called the transept. The large, flat book was still on the table, light reflecting off its white pages.

"I'm supposed to read this book," she said. "At least, I *think* this is the book I'm supposed to read. I'm guessing it has instructions or something, like the prophecy from this summer. The problem is, it's completely blank! And then I…well, I asked a question. And…"

Her fingers went to her ring, and she looked up at the Elizabethan portrait on the wall. Jaye's and Hayley's faces weren't there anymore; it was just two prim-looking women in funny collars now. Beneath the painting was a plaque that read LADIES OF THE COURT.

"Anyway, the answer was you guys," she said after a

moment. "I think you're supposed to help me read the book."

Hayley stared at her.

"You called us out in Boston in the middle of the night to *read* a *book*?" she said. "Are you *serious*?"

"I *have* to, or I won't know how to get to my mother," said Cara quietly. "It's—just like it was in August. I need her again. And if I can't find her, I won't be able to help Jax."

"You said he was *poisoned*?" asked Hayley. "So is he like in the *hospital* now? And where is everyone? How come this place is so empty?"

"Long story," said Cara. "Later, promise."

She leaned over the book, and the other two followed suit. Jaye touched the corner of one of the huge pages, then turned it gingerly. They saw the next page was blank, too. Hayley grabbed some pages at the end and opened the book there: still nothing.

"So what exactly are we supposed to do?"

"Maybe we need to hold a light to it. Remember when we were little, how there was this way you could do invisible ink using lemon juice?" asked Jaye. "You could write with the juice, and it didn't show up on the paper. But then the writing would turn brown when you held it up to a light bulb, and you could read it?"

"Uh, *I* never did that," said Hayley.

"Too busy with Fashionista Barbie," said Jaye. "Here, I'll hold this side."

They maneuvered the book in close to the green reading lamp and tried their best to peer over at the page.

Nothing.

Hayley peeled off her jacket and plunked it down on the table; Cara pushed up her sleeves. Was it getting even hotter, she wondered? Were they coming?

"I guess it might have to do with my ring," she said.

"That good-luck ring?" asked Hayley.

"Maybe I have to ask a question again, but with the two of you here. I see these pictures, if I touch the ring. Sometimes. I don't quite know how it works. My mom called them visions."

She touched the ring and leaned toward the book, sandwiched closely between her friends. She thought: *How do we read you?*

And it seemed to her that she was just beginning to notice something shift on the white page, almost like one of those fractals rearranging itself, when Jaye shrieked.

Cara looked up—Hayley was grabbing at her—to see fire. It was leaping on the hotplate in the corner, where Mrs. O had boiled the water for her tea; an actual fire was burning there, crinkling the tablecloth, sparks and pieces of burning fabric fluttering toward the floor.

It was a small fire, at least, and Cara thought maybe she could put it out. She'd put out a fire once before when Jax, age eight, decided to conduct combustion experiments with household cleaning products. So she rushed over, looking for something to use and thinking randomly of a TV show where a man set on fire had been rolled up in a rug to quench the flames; she grabbed the corner of the Persian rug beneath her feet and pulled it up, then brought it down clumsily on the burning tabletop.

As soon as she had it on top of the flames, though, the rug got heavy in her hands. The rug seemed lumpy. Heavier and heavier, and then suddenly there was movement, the rug was resisting her, and the fire leapt up instead of subsiding as she thought it should. Vaguely aware of her friends screaming behind her, she had to jump back—because the rug was hot, and the rug *had something inside it.*

She dropped it, her hands hurting, but was barely aware of the pain because now she was looking at the man from the subway, rising out of the lumps in the rug, and he opened his mouth and his mouth was flames.

## Five

*It wasn't only him, either.*

Behind the Burner, as Cara and her friends backed up, others appeared—all of them copies, as though he was duplicating himself. They had the same face. They all opened their mouths in the same way, and in every single wide-open mouth the orange tongues of fire flickered. And then they were coming forward, and heat blasted off them in a wave.

Fear hit Cara along with the heat, but oddly she found she was thinking clearly. She had to get the book. It *had* to be the right one; she'd seen it start to respond to them. She grabbed it off the table but instantly dropped it—her hands hurt too much to hold on, a searing agony on the palms. The rug had burned them.

"Get the book!" she yelled to the others, and Jaye leaned down and grabbed it and then they were running. The three of them ran as fast as they could, through the thick drapes on the door, swerving down the hall the way they'd come in….

But the heat didn't let up. The heat stayed right at their backs. It wasn't that the Burners were running, just that they were *there*—there were no thudding footsteps but those of the girls themselves, no noise but a low crackle—the crackle of flame—and a rhythmic sound like heavy breathing. Heat pulsed from them, heat pushed at Cara's head and shoulders and forced her to run fast, pell-mell along the corridors, banging against cabinets and statues as she went.

How could they get away? They had to go somewhere the Burners couldn't go.

"We've got to get into the cold!" she yelled.

Outside it was cold, she thought, and the Burners didn't like cold. Would they follow the girls into the elevator? Could they? She didn't know where the stairs even were, in the core, and anyway this was the eighth floor…so they couldn't make it that far. They couldn't *make* it all the way outside.

Then she remembered the kitchen. It was near, and it had a walk-in fridge. Or maybe freezer. She'd passed it as they went into dinner: a door with a small window and the kind of metal handle you sometimes pulled up to open an airtight door, even a sign that read COLD STORAGE PLEASE CLOSE TILL IT CLICKS.

"This way," she cried out, and had to push Hayley to make a turn. She thought she knew the way—it was down some stairs, but not too many, she thought—and then, running, she realized there was too much heat on her back now. Too much to stand. Something was burning.

It was her fleece hoodie. She knew it wasn't the shirt, because her skin wasn't hurting. Yet. She shrugged desperately as she ran, frantically, and the burning hoodie fell behind, but now the shirt beneath it felt, hot too—

"Hot," came a breathy, raspy voice, almost right in her ear. "Hot…hot…hot…"

It wasn't either of the other girls, who were beside her and in front. It was him.

"Turn! Down the stairs!" she cried out, and they did, stumbling as they fell against each other. She smelled something acrid and was suddenly afraid of her hair catching fire. Her whole body felt weak. They were scrambling against the wall, their feet were slipping on the stone, and then there was the kitchen door. They banged through it.

"Left! Left!" she yelled, and Jaye grabbed the door to the cold-storage room. And jerked it open.

"Hot…" breathed the voice, beside her.

And then they were inside, tripping over each other and a pile of big cardboard boxes right in the middle of the floor. The big book, which Jaye had been carrying, snagged the edge of a shelf and fell onto the floor; frigid air hit their dripping faces, and Cara turned and slammed the door shut.

The Burners were black now, their features almost gone except for the bright mouth-holes—the skin cracked and wrinkled and burnt up.

❧

"Oh my *God!*" burst out Jaye as they sat on the boxes huffing and puffing.

Cara was glad this wasn't a walk-in freezer but only a fridge—lucky for them. She held her hands out in front of her. They were shockingly pink and raw.

"I can't believe this," said Hayley.

"It's crazy," said Jaye, shaking her head.

"I'm sorry," said Cara, staring at her trembling hands. "I'm so, so sorry I got you into this."

"Those look bad," said Hayley.

"You need cold water—right away," said Jaye. "Is there water in here?"

They were being practical, Cara realized, in order to stop thinking of the Burners. She felt grateful.

Hayley got up and started scanning the long shelves, already shivering in the cold.

"There's drinking water," she said, and reached for a bottle.

"If we don't have running water, we need a towel," said Jaye. "To make a cold compress. That's second best."

"The only sink's out there," said Cara, gritting her teeth at the pain. "We can't risk going out yet."

"Are they just *waiting*?" asked Hayley.

"Look," said Jaye, "here."

There was a blue-and-white dishtowel hanging from a hook; Jaye grabbed it and poured water onto it from the bottle Hayley handed her.

"I hope it's clean," she said, and then gently laid the wet cloth over Cara's hands. "You have to keep it there a while."

The coolness felt good at first, but the towel was also scratchy and the textured loops of thread started to feel like they were stabbing the sensitive skin if she moved her hands even a little. Cara bit her lip and sat looking down at her trembling arms. Her heart was still beating too fast.

"You're gonna be OK," said Jaye gently, kneeling down beside her. "It's only first degree. I'm almost sure. There aren't any blisters yet, at least."

"Cara. What the hell *were* those things?" said Hayley.

She unscrewed a second bottle of water and glugged from it.

"They're called elementals," said Cara. She was trying to keep from crying, the burns hurt so much; talking slowly and deliberately seemed to help. It kept her focused on something other than her hands. "They're not human."

"Hmm, really," said Hayley, and swallowed a big gulp. "No kidding. Those things were like CGI. They were walking special effects."

"Too bad they don't keep aspirin in here," said Jaye.

Looking up from her hands, Cara saw Hayley's eyebrows were singed, the top hairs black and curling, and some stray hairs on her head, too. It must have been burning hair she smelled.

Hayley put her hand up, seeing Cara's gaze rest there, and touched her eyebrows; the burnt ends came off on her fingers. She stared at them. For a long moment Cara had the distinct sensation that all three of them were in an unreality; they would wake up, like people did in a bad movie, and all of this would turn out to be a dream.

"I don't know what the elementals *are*, exactly," she went on, shaking it off and wincing as one of her hands shifted and the tender skin scraped painfully on the towel. "But they work for this guy called the Cold One, or just the Cold.

There are four kinds. The Pouring Man was a water elemental, which meant he needed water to move around in. There had to be some form of water for him to show up in a place. These guys are fire, obviously. They need fire or at least heat. It's the four elements, the ancient elements—remember that Classics unit we had in History? So there must be others, too. Earth and air, I guess."

"Huh," said Hayley. "Earth, that seems kind of lame. Like what are they going to do, scare us with potted plants?"

Cara tried to laugh at that, but she could barely crack a smile.

"How about *air*," said Jaye. "I mean, if some move through water, and some through fire, they have some major limits, right? But air is everywhere. We *breathe* it. I wouldn't want to meet up with those guys."

They sat in silence for a minute. Cara looked up at her friends; they looked small and…well, unsure of themselves. Anyone would be, she thought, and this was just *them*, three girls in junior high and those blackened things outside the door.

"Listen," she said. "What we need to do is get out of the building, right? I'm pretty sure it's too cold for them in the night air."

"But they could be *out* there," said Jaye. "Right outside the fridge door. That window is too small, even if it weren't all fogged up. How could we even tell if they left?"

"I'm going to try to find out," said Cara.

She could use the nazar, at least.

She looked down at the towel, a field of nubbly blue and white over her trembling hands.

"Jaye," she said, "can you take the towel off? I mean, really slowly?"

Jaye shook her head. "We shouldn't lift it. Not yet. Give it five more minutes."

"OK. But then we have to make a move."

"Eee-yeah. And what move would that be?" asked Hayley.

Cara shook her head. She was going to figure this out; they weren't going to be stuck in here. Her mother was imprisoned; her baby brother was imprisoned, because that wasn't him behind those eyes. She refused to be trapped, too.

"What did they *want* from us?" asked Jaye.

Cara remembered the book. She'd almost forgotten it, preoccupied with the pain shooting across her palms. She turned her head carefully and looked down.

Jaye and Hayley had to pick it up, since Cara couldn't use her hands yet. They lifted the big, empty book and placed it on a box in front of her; they opened it together, one on each side of her.

Beneath the wet towel, Cara raised one shaking hand over the other, palms still up, and very gently touched her ring. Just with a fingernail.

She closed her eyes and pictured her mother, thinking the question: *Where is she?* She thought of nothing else, just her mother. It was hard at first because trying to think of

her mother made her think of herself *missing* her mother…
which she knew was wrong. She had to think more clearly
than that. So one by one she pulled up memories of her
mother. There she was when Cara was very young, smiling down with a paper mobile of seagulls behind her head;
there she was at school when Cara was in first grade, putting
Cara's lunchbox in a cubby, smiling at another mother over
Cara's head. She always seemed to have been smiling then.

Cara remembered that smile and focused on it. *Where
is she? Where is my mother?*

And when she opened her eyes again, the white of the
pages was moving like snow drifting across an Arctic landscape, or clouds passing each other with faint shadings of
gray in the white. It was beautiful. All three of them stared;
Jaye gasped.

Dark colors flared onto the page. They washed across
it, unfurling into a moving scene as detailed and vivid as
a high-def screen. It was night and there was a huge gray-
black building with a few small lights in windows and mul-
tiple smokestacks sticking into the night sky like pillars.
There were also massive white towers that reminded Cara
of old pictures of nuclear disasters, wide at the bottom and
curving in and then out again as they rose.

"Oh my God," breathed Hayley.

"A factory?" asked Cara.

"Actually, I think it's a power plant," said Jaye.

So they could see it, too. It wasn't one of her visions. Or
at least, it wasn't *only* that.

"But it's—is it *animation*?" said Hayley. "What is it?"

Then Cara noticed the edges of the book were also changing. They didn't look like book pages anymore; the paper and binding faded.

What they looked like was a window frame.

"Um. It seems to be turning into a *window*," said Jaye.

And there was something about the picture: it wasn't a picture. It wasn't 2D at all.

"Touch it," whispered Cara to Jaye.

Jaye tentatively reached out her hand.

There was space there. Her hand didn't knock up against anything. She jerked it back.

"Just—space," she said, awed.

"That's how we get away," said Cara. "We go there."

"*Go* there?" asked Hayley.

"It's where my mother's being held," said Cara. "That was the question that I asked."

"This is scary," said Hayley, and sat heavily down on a box. "It's way too weird."

"We have to go," said Cara. "Even if I brought up a different place, the only way for us to get away from these guys is through"—she pointed down at the window that had once been a book—"this right here."

"You want us to step into some kind of window that—that isn't really there?"

"We don't know where that place even *is*," said Jaye. "It could be Afghanistan. It could be *anywhere*."

"We have to," said Cara. "It's what we're supposed to do."

"That's all you got?" asked Hayley. "We're *supposed* to? That's messed *up*. It makes me feel queasy."

"Look," said Jaye, in a grim tone.

She was pointing at the refrigerator door.

At the small window in the door, glass white with steam. It seemed to be *melting*—melting and trailing in grayish lumps down the metal.

Cara watched a stream of it race down the door's inside. It hissed and sizzled like drops of water hitting a hot stove.

"Hold my arms," she said, and stood.

She was above the open book that had turned into a window. She still had the wet cloth on her hands.

"Grab my arms!' she urged, when her friends didn't move. "*Now.*"

She felt them clutching her upper arms (even *that* hurt her hands as they moved against the rough cloth of the towel), but she squeezed her eyes shut and raised one foot and stepped forward into nothingness.

It was like falling. No: it *was* falling. Her stomach flipped, and she wanted to yell in terror: she was stepping off a ledge into thin air—down, down, with no idea how it would end.

Then it did. Her feet made contact with a solid, flat surface: she was hitting the ground. She held her hands up reflexively, held them out and fell onto her elbows instead; that hurt, too. But not anything like as badly as the burns.

They were on an expanse of dried-out, brown grass. Strewn through the grass were the white smudges of cigarette butts, dirty Styrofoam cups, and crushed soda cans in the tangle of weeds. In front of them was a high, chain-link fence with razor wire curling on top; behind it was the massive power plant.

Wherever they were, it wasn't Narnia.

But they were safe from the Burners, anyway. At least for now.

She sat up. Hayley groaned beside her, and Jaye kicked at Cara's shin by mistake, struggling to get upright.

Off to their left there were what looked like low, black hills—piles of powdered coal, Cara realized—along with a big A-frame building made of metal. There were long chutes going up and down between buildings farther off, and a row of freight cars sitting on a railroad track. Off to the right was a row of tall lights, which shone brightly over water that glittered in large, square ponds with banks of cement.

"That was amazing!" squeaked Jaye, breathless. "I can't believe that—that happened to me! Is it—Cara, seriously—is it *magic*? Is that what it is?"

"I don't know," said Cara honestly. "I don't know how it works."

"What matters is we're in the middle of nowhere," said Hayley, brushing dirt off her clothes as she stood up.

"Or at least, at a coal-fired power plant," amended Jaye. "In the middle of nowhere."

Cara looked up at the fence with its sharp wire.

"Would have been nice," she admitted, "if the book had put us *inside* that."

The *book*, she thought, and looked around in a panic.

And there it was, on the ground behind them. Looking like nothing special—just a big, flat book with a dark cover.

Hopefully they could use it again, thought Cara. To get back.

"This place is huge," said Hayley. "How are we supposed to find your mom in there? It's the size of, like, a small city."

"One step at a time. We just have to trust the flow," said Cara.

"Rad," said Hayley. "Next you'll be telling me what color my aura is."

"I mean the flow of events—like we have to take it one step at a time," said Cara. "First we need to find an opening in the fence. Because even if we *could* make it over the razors, I can't climb with my hands like this. Can one of you guys carry the book again?"

Jaye leaned down to pick it up.

Left or right? Cara didn't know. She touched the nazar again, her hands still shaky though the pain was starting to ebb a little, and tried to ask it for a picture, but all she got was a faint urge to go left instead of right. In fact, she couldn't tell if the urge was something she was making up or something that was real. But nothing more definite occurred to her, so she decided she might as well go with it.

"This way," she said, trying to sound confident.

They skirted the chain-link fence in the dark. Hayley was right: it was uncomfortable not to know where they were. They could be anywhere—anywhere it was fall right now, anyway, anywhere that had power plants—and that gave Cara an unmoored feeling, as though the place was only half-there. The night world was huge, and somewhere in that darkness, cut loose from everything they knew and everyone who knew them, she and her two best friends crept over the surface as tiny as ants.

If Jax were with them, she thought, he'd use his GPS in a way she could never use hers. (Jax could do things with his phone she didn't hope to understand.) He'd tell her right away how far it was to the nearest bus stop, the nearest gas station or all-night diner. Probably even the nearest bathroom.

And if Max were here, he'd make a joke or two and she wouldn't have to feel like success or failure was all on her. Her friends were here, and they were great, but she'd brought them into this and it would be her fault if anything happened to them.

She realized she was truly relieved it was her hands that had got burned, not anyone else's.

"Look!" said Jaye. "There!"

Sure enough, the fence was ripped; part of it had been pried away from one of the metal posts that connected its sections, and there was a long, thin triangular opening.

"So much for Homeland Security," said Hayley, whose mother was almost as interested in terrorists as she was in kidnappers and perverts. "Someone could just walk in and plant a bomb or whatever. We could be Al Qaeda. The nation is, like, completely lucky it's just us."

They bent down, Jaye holding the book sideways, and one by one they ducked through.

"Are there guards?" asked Jaye, and answered her own question. "There have to be guards. And cameras and all that. If they catch us, they'll definitely not let us in."

They saw the long, bright stripe of a searchlight slowly sweeping the ground around the outside of the main building, originating from somewhere up on the roof. It disappeared at the far end of the complex, to their right, and then rotated around and started up again at the left.

"I don't know if we can stay hidden," said Cara. "I think that light moves faster than we can."

"We'll have to try to outrun it," said Jaye. "What else can we do?"

"Just don't drop that book thing, Jaye," warned Hayley. "I really don't want to get stuck here."

Cara watched the beam scope across the lake of cement stretching before them.

"We wait till the leading end of the light passes us, then make a dash for it," she decided. "And cross our fingers we get to the building before it starts up again. Let's aim for that double door, OK?"

She raised an aching hand and pointed.

As they waited for the searchlight to finish its circuit and begin again, she closed her eyes and touched the ring. *Where is she?* she thought. *Where in the power plant? Where? Where?*

And then she saw something: pipes stretching across a floor, with a grid of wooden slats beneath them. Something clouding the air. But Hayley's voice interrupted.

"*Go! Now!*"

Her friends were already running, and the beam was moving off to her right. The vision had only seemed to last a second, but she must have been standing there for longer without being aware of time passing.... She sprinted after them, arms rigid at her side to keep her hands from flopping around more than they had to. She could feel the blood throbbing in her fingers, making her more conscious of the soreness. *Just get to the doors*, she told herself, *just make it to the doors, and then we'll be out of the searchlight's scope....*

She was catching up to Jaye, she realized, who was running a little slower than Hayley since she had the book under one arm; over the hard ground, first on dried grass, then on concrete. She was dimly aware of some machinery off to the left, more chutes or silos or something, silent and angular in one corner of the lot; then the doors loomed.

"It's coming around again!" yelled Jaye, and they picked up their pace and then jerked to a stop to avoid slamming against the wall of the building. A bright white light glared over their heads, then left them in the dark again. Or not quite dark—there were other lights on the building itself—but Cara didn't see anyone around who might notice them.

They stood panting, Cara's hands trembling again and tears standing on the rims of her eyes, whether from the force of the air as she ran or from the pain in her hands she couldn't quite figure out.

"Made it," breathed Hayley.

"So far so good," said Jaye, and Cara contented herself with a brief nod as she tried to still the shaking.

They listened, expecting the sound of an alarm to pierce the night, but none came. Cara focused again on what she'd seen: an empty room. Pipes. Water spraying from them onto a wooden lattice below.

"Jaye," she said when she caught her breath. "Do you know anything about the inside of places like this?"

Jaye shook her head.

"My dad took me to a plant once," she said. "That old one in Sandwich, right before the bridge. But I was really little. Why?"

"I think my mother's in a room with water," said Cara.

"There's lots of water in power plants," said Jaye. "That could be anywhere."

"Water is spraying down," said Cara. "All these little nozzles are coming out of pipes, and water is spraying down from them. Then, beneath that, there was a kind of wooden grid…."

"I'm thinking," frowned Jaye. "But it was so long ago. I'm *trying* to remember…."

"It sounds like a cooling tower," said Hayley suddenly.

Both of them looked at her, surprised.

"A cooling tower?" asked Cara.

"Yeah, how those things look inside," said Hayley, and pointed in the direction of the two hourglass-curved giants that hulked over the complex. They had to be hundreds of feet tall, Cara thought. "My mom had this boyfriend last year who was a lineman for NStar—"

"You never told me about that," said Cara reflexively.

"Yeah, well, it lasted ten seconds. Anyway, he was a lineman and really macho and proud of it. One time he tried to do the bonding-with-the-kid thing, hunkered down at my computer and made me take a virtual tour. It was wicked boring. Not the Canal plant—it was one on the mainland. Those towers are basically empty except for the water that gets sprayed at the bottom. The big white clouds coming out are called plumes."

Would the Burners keep her mother in a *cool* place? Cara wondered. A place with water, where they apparently couldn't go?

"It's really cool you knew that, Hay," she said.

"Whatever. The guy like basically *forced* me to do this uber-boring tour."

But even in the meager half-light cast across her friend's face, Cara could tell Hayley was pleased by the compliment.

"Then let's bounce," said Jaye.

Hugging the wall of the building, they moved toward the massive towers, which were sometimes visible if they craned their necks and sometimes out of view. Jaye went first, and then Hayley and Cara. There was a hum coming from inside the building—what Cara guessed was the hum of power being generated. But other than that they heard only the soft noises of their footsteps, the brush of their clothes against the wall.

Abruptly, Cara had a sense of discomfort. It seemed to come from nowhere and grow quickly. She kept moving, but as she moved she touched the ring again. *Is there a danger here?* she thought, and blinked her eyes quickly. She couldn't afford to stand still or lose time.

But she saw nothing.

Try again.

*What is the danger to us here?*

Again she blinked. And this time she did see—for a moment.

It was one of the cooling towers, and outside it there were people standing. Encircling the base in a human chain—a ring of them looking outward, guarding like toy soldiers with their hands clasped in front of them and their feet splayed. They weren't Burners, or if they were, they were nothing like the bland man from the subway train with his army of clones. They looked like regular people, almost relaxed except for the fact that they all stood the same way. Not security guards, though, because as far as she could tell they weren't wearing uniforms. And because…

Because some of them were kids. Some of them were children. Children of different ages.

Just as she realized that the picture vanished.

"Stop. *Stop*," she hissed to Hayley and Jaye.

They were about to round the corner of the building, and it was possible they would be in view.

Both of them froze.

She leaned a shoulder against the wall to steady herself.

"Wait a minute," she whispered, and closed her eyes again.

Yes. There were children, along with women and men. Some of the kids looked even younger than Jax, while some were older than she was. They were dressed as any kids might be, and yet there was something abnormal about them.

It was the eyes. The eyes...their pupils were like Jax's. They were large and blacker than black, not convex but so concave that it seemed they had no bottom. They were empty; the eyes seemed to have holes in them, holes of an endless depth.

※

The three of them hunched at the corner, whispering.

"Maybe we should just go home," suggested Jaye when Cara told them about the people with huge black eyes. "I mean—get help. Cara, you got *hurt*. By guys who *breathed fire*. And I bet even worse things could happen—"

"No *way*," interrupted Hayley, and shook her head.

It occurred to Cara that Hayley was more confident since she'd figured out about the cooling towers.

"Seriously," went on Hayley, "I *can't* go back right now. I've gotta have something to show for all this. Like Jax. A rescued kid might be my only get-out-of-jail-free card. The crap I'll be in with my mom? A bunch of stoners standing around a giant water cooler is like *no sweat* compared to that."

"Um, I don't think they're stoned," said Cara grimly.

"You know that stoner dude in tenth grade? Muller? He couldn't guard his way out of a paper bag. He just drags his feet around and drones on about fractals and Phish."

"They're not stoners," insisted Cara. "I know they have the dilated pupils. But I promise you it's not drugs. Or at least not the kind you mean."

"My point is, we went to all this trouble to get here. We should finish. Even if we never tell my mom. I mean, best case she never notices we're gone."

"But we can't get *past* the people," said Jaye. "We're outnumbered. I mean, even if we got by them, which is assuming the door's open and we can even *find* it before they grab us, they'd just come in, too."

"We have to get in without them *knowing*," said Cara.

"Can we use the book again?" asked Hayley. "And just, like, be beamed in there?"

"It's worth a try," said Cara. "Except...I don't know, but something tells me there's a reason it didn't take us there in the first place."

"Let's just try anyway," said Hayley, and Jaye knelt and opened the book on the ground. The three of them squatted down around it.

"We have to be touching," said Cara. "It takes all three of us, I think."

124

With both of them pressed close against her sides, she moved one hand over the other to touch the nazar and stared down at the book, thinking *We want to go inside. Inside the guarded tower.*

She was hoping for a scene of the inside of the cooling tower, like what she'd gotten when she asked, back in the refrigerated room at the Institute, where her mother was. She waited for it to wash across the page the way the scene of the power plant had.

But the pages stayed snowy white.

*Please, book, take us inside*, she begged. *We can't face… those people. Whoever or whatever they may be. Take us past them. Take us inside.*

Nothing.

Maybe the book had simply taken them as far as it could. Maybe there were wards here, or something. That had to be it, she thought. It had brought them as far as it could. But if the book could take you places, she wondered, could it bring *others* to the place where *you* were? Could it bring her something that could transport them?

She stared down at the pages again. *If we can't go in*, she thought, *then bring us something that can take us—take us into the place where my mother is.*

*Bring us transportation.*

And then the white shifted. It happened fast this time, so fast she couldn't follow the image at all as it came up—a muddy swirl was all she saw. She felt a rush of air, and then it was on them: the book was still lying on the cement, but something was emerging from it, dark and huge with an impossibly long, straight beak.

The beak alone was far longer than her arm.

They jumped up—she thought she heard Hayley yell— and stumbled back. Cara fell down, and before she could stop herself she broke the fall with her hands, which shot a searing pang up her arms.

The thing coming out of the book was monstrous. It had wings and four legs, not two like a bird. Its long head, which seemed to be all beak, was too far up to see clearly. It had scales, or at least a leathery hide that might be tiny scales or might be something else. It stood over them clawing the ground and stretching its wings, dark and smelling strongly of something she couldn't name—maybe sweat, maybe dust. Maybe both. It was larger than a horse—had a wingspan, she thought, that must be three times her father's height at least.

She remembered her mother leaving them in their backyard, and Jax saying *It looked like a pterosaur.*

"Get on!" she called to the others, though her jaw ached from clenching her teeth at the pain in her hands. She struggled to her feet. "This guy's our *ride!*"

She clambered on quickly, trying to use her elbows but having to grab with her hands once or twice, painfully. The others were white-faced, too off balance to even whisper. The pterosaur was bony on top, bony and too dark to see over the neck to the head—the neck was thin and the body narrow—and there wasn't much room on its back because most of its bulk was wing. When she made it to the top and threw one leg over, she had to grab desperately with the muscles on the insides of her thighs, recalling a horse-riding lesson she'd once had.

But it was much harder than riding a horse because the bird was stringy and bony, and her bent legs stretched out in an ungainly way over the parts of the beast where the wings sprang from the rib cage. There wasn't room behind the wings, either, because now Jaye and Hayley were struggling to get on, and if Cara tried to climb farther up she'd be directly over the base of the narrow neck, which was far too thin to balance on.

"You holding on?" she yelled, fumbling at the textured hide for handholds. Her aching fingers were stiff and crooked as crab claws. She scrabbled to get a grip: all she could find were bony ridges to clutch—shoulder blades, possibly, striking out at angles from her perch.

She couldn't hear what her friends answered, though Hayley's arms were clutching at her waist; then the creature's long beak swung around toward them, at an almost impossible angle. It reared up close to their heads, and they shrank back. Cara couldn't see teeth—maybe it was toothless—but still, it looked razor-sharp.

As it turned out, all the beak did was gently nudge—nudge at Hayley and Jaye. Nudge them backwards.

"Oh. I think," said Cara, with a glimmer of understanding, "it can't carry all of us at once. It's too light, or we're too heavy…. I think it means you guys should step down because we have to take turns."

So Hayley and Jaye scrambled back down, and the wings flapped as the pterosaur's long front legs bent; then there was a jerky bounce-like movement, and Cara gasped as she and the beast lifted.

They glided for a while above the parking lot and then over a stretch of dead grass before the creature suddenly banked—Cara tightened her legs and fingers to hold on—and rose steeply.

*Why does it have to fly so* high? she thought.

Because instead of flying straight for the cooling tower the winged creature had veered away from it, up into the night, ascending higher and higher. She had to clutch hard with her hands; if she fell, she thought, she couldn't possibly survive.

The tender, burnt skin of her palms felt as though it was about to rip open.

*We can't be seen*, she thought. *That's why.*

That had to be it: the beast needed a flight path that protected it—and her—from all those pairs of dark eyes. Yes: the beast intended to rise so high that, instead of coasting in from the side, where the watchers might pick it out against the sky, it could hover way above the great open mouth of the tower and then come *plummeting hundreds of feet straight down.*

She wouldn't be able to hold on, she thought, as they soared higher and higher. How could she hold on if the beast dropped straight down? She *couldn't*. She'd tumble forward over its head and probably break her neck on impact, as well as every other bone in her body. The beast couldn't know her hands were burnt; it couldn't know she'd have more than the usual trouble hanging on in a steep dive like that.

She needed something to hold on *with*, she thought. She needed reins.

She had no reins. Needless to say.

All she had was a belt. She never wore belts, but for some reason she'd put one on today....

She had to get it off *now*, she thought, before it was too late; so she let go of the shoulder-bone with her right hand and fumbled to unhook it from the loops on her jeans. It was a leather belt with a magnetic clasp, so it slid out easily with one hand, and she was glad. Would it be strong enough?

She leaned forward, still holding a shoulder bone with her left hand, and thought about how she could loop it around the neck, loop and tie....

The tower was almost below them. From above it just looked like a huge, perfectly round hole, though misted over in parts by the plume.

She'd never been afraid of heights before. But now she was. Terrified, in fact.

She had to tie the belt on.

*It's now or never*, she thought. *Now*!

So she let go with her left hand, too, and leaned forward and down, pressed against the base of the neck, which moved up and down slightly. Eyes closed, she lowered the belt and reached around from beneath to grab the other end. Palms smarting, teeth clenched, she forced herself to tie the belt at the top, though it was stiff and her fingers trembled. Hopefully when she pulled hard it wouldn't strangle the creature....

She pulled it tighter and tighter, pressing her thighs and knees so hard into the sides of the creature, the wing bases, that she worried she might hurt it.

And then it hovered.

And dove.

She kept her eyes squeezed shut, her whole body tensed up, every muscle and tendon straining to cling to the bony frame. The wings seemed hardly to be moving, folded back somehow as the pterosaur plunged. She held on as tightly as she could, and still it was all she could do not to fall off—her body wanted to hurtle forward, and the belt, though it gave her something to pull against, wasn't tight enough to anchor her. She tried to put all her strength in the muscles of her thighs, pressing, pressing....

Because of her squeezed-shut eyes it was a dark, headlong rush down, and she didn't know how long it was going to last and tried not to think about it—till abruptly she felt the pterosaur stretch its wings out again, start to right its body—and then the flight ended.

Because she did fall, after all.

Luckily, only a few feet.

She landed on a kind of narrow sidewalk, hit the wall, scraped her knees and elbows, and was shocked by the sudden release.

When she collected herself and the dizziness started to recede—enough for her to sit up and glance at the torn cloth and scrapes on her elbows—she saw she'd fetched up on a thin walkway that circled the roomy inside of the tower, enclosing a grid of pipes and sprayers with wooden slats beneath them. The wall she was leaning against was soaking wet and covered in material that reminded her of roof shingles after a long rain. Cool air rushed around her; she wasn't sure where from. It blew her hair into strings, stuck the strings against her mouth and into her eyes, and made her shiver.

The beast was already flapping toward the sky; possibly it had never even landed, had just dumped her and swooped up again. She wondered if it *was* going to bring her friends to join her. Maybe not; maybe it would just return to whatever mysterious place it had come from.

As she watched it get smaller and smaller in the circle of sky above her, she felt lucky; she could have broken a leg. Or worse. She stood up, creaky, and looked around. Where was her mother? She saw no one at all. There was only the loud, constant *whoosh* of water spraying from the pipes, hundreds of tiny nozzles releasing water downward from the pipes to the slats, and the confusion of the wind.

It seemed like the emptiest place she'd ever been.

Her vision must have been wrong.

A fog rose from the water; low lights made it possible to make out a few shapes in the cavernous space, but it was dim and murky. She smelled something chemical, possibly chlorine covering up other, worse smells—mold? Rot? There was another walkway a few feet away, crossing the grid of pipes and wood lattice below it. Still a bit off-kilter. She stepped onto the walkway, her arms outstretched though it was a good couple of feet wide—not too precarious for someone her size. She had to look around, no matter how hopeless it seemed; she might not have much time before the people with black eyes found out that she was here. And then what—would the pterosaur come back for her? Was she trapped? Again?

As her eyes adjusted she could make out doors in the tower walls, metal doors, and at one end there seemed to be steps down from a platform, a kind of scaffolding, a little above floor level....

She gazed down at the spraying water, then around at the walls. If her mother was here, she thought, she had to be on that platform; there was nowhere else a person could hide. And yet the platform didn't have real walls, just a kind of skeleton of wood. She didn't see anywhere her mother could be hiding.

And then something splashed, down beneath her feet.
*Cara! Cara!*
But she wasn't hearing it with her ears.
"Mom?"
There was an echo effect in the chamber: *Mom—Mom—Mom*...until it died away.

*Down here. Beneath.*

She looked down from the walkway. All she could see was the steadily spraying water, the soaked wooden planks.

*I'm here. In the basin.*

"How can you be?" she asked aloud.

*Beneath the pipes and beneath the wood is water in a basin. I'm swimming in it. I had to take another form.*

"What do you mean, another form?"

*This is going to be hard to hear, honey. It's something I can do. I change from form to form, if I need to.*

"But then—what you do—is it that shapeshifting thing?"

*Yes.*

Cara didn't speak for a while, watching the spray.

"So then—so what *are* you?"

*Last summer, for instance, I was the sea otter. Now I'm a fish.*

## Six

*It was ridiculous. And yet Cara found she actually believed it*—or more, even: about the sea otter, part of her had already known.

She knelt at the edge of the walkway, staring down. All she saw was the mist of the sprayers, the wet wood.

"But, Mom. I mean, how can you *do* that and still be..."

She trailed off. The rest of what she thought was *human*? But she couldn't bring herself to say it out loud.

Then it came: *It's complicated. I'm sorry—I know it's hard to get your mind around. Even* your *mind, which is resilient. But listen, this water's pretty toxic. I need to get out soon.*

"How can hear me all the way up here?"

*I can hear you with my mind. What brought you here, sweetie? Are you safe?*

"Jax isn't. He got poisoned. By Roger from your work."

*Roger! Roger?—Roger.*

The word came to Cara with a tone of disbelief; then tightly controlled fury.

"It wasn't normal poison," she added. "It was something else. And the people taking care of him, the teachers at the

Institute, told me to get a memory from you—to bring back a memory for them to fix him with."

*Roger. I can't believe it. They needed someone close to me—*

"Mom. Listen! There are people outside with these black eyes. Like Jax has. They're going to know I'm in here soon. So would you tell me what to do?"

*They hollowed him out.*

And then, colder: *I am going to kill that man.*

"*Mom.* Can you stop obsessing? What should I do?"

*See if you can break the wooden slats. I could do it myself, if I were in my first form, but I can't do it as a fish. Break some of them for me.*

Cara paused, then walked toward the opposite wall, searching the shadows for objects—anything that would split wood. Even a rake, she thought, or a shovel...but of course there was nothing like that here. She couldn't do it with her hands; for one thing, it was far down, out of her reach, so that if she leaned over enough to touch it she'd fall in. She needed something long and heavy.

She could stamp the slats and pipes with her feet, she was thinking, if only she had something up here to hold on to, when she heard the flap of wings and a high, keening sound. She glanced up to see the pterosaur descending, a big, brown blur. She realized the sound was coming from Jaye, who was clinging to the thing's neck—Cara's belt, in fact—for dear life with her eyes shut, just as Cara had, and trying to suppress a scream.

And then she was unceremoniously tipped off the beast's back—again, just like Cara. She rolled along the walkway a bit, hitting one foot on a pipe.

"Wait!" yelled Cara, catching sight of the creature's impossibly long beak as it started to rise again. "Don't leave—we need you! We really need your help!"

Flap, flap.

After an instant of what seemed like hesitation, it landed and perched on the walkway, arranging itself precariously with its five-taloned claws gripping both edges of the catwalk and its great wings half spread, slightly vibrating.

She could see the head a lot better now that she wasn't sitting above it. The beak was yellow and brown, and there was a protrusion on the back of its skull, like a crest; the eyes were tiny, barely visible, and the neck was hairy. The creature was less scary than homely and bizarre—except for the fact that it couldn't possibly exist.

That part *was* a little unnerving.

"Do you *understand*? When I talk?" she asked.

The thing cocked its head. It reminded her of a dog.

"If you do—we have to break the wooden slats there. See? We need to make a hole big enough for a person to get through. Could you—?"

It lunged forward with its massive beak—Cara jumped back, almost losing her balance. The beak poked past her, down between the pipes, and she heard a splintering sound as the creature made a series of vicious-looking jabs. She shuddered, imagining what that beak could do to her own tender skin.

She turned to Jaye, sitting against the wall staring.

"Are you OK?" she yelled over the racket.

Jaye shook her head and pointed to her ears. The sound of breaking wood was loud over the background noise of the sprayers, and then there was the echo. All this had to be audible from outside, Cara realized with a jolt of alarm. Didn't it?

Were those black eyes widening now, those blank-faced people turning and filing toward the doors?

There were no windows, and the metal doors appeared locked tight, but still—it was so loud...

The pterosaur made a strange, squawking croak, then flapped its wings and was airborne again.

It had succeeded. It had broken a section of pipe as well as the network of wood planks beneath: water rushed out, and Cara couldn't easily see beyond it. In the distance she heard a beeping. An alarm. Time was ticking away.

"Mom!" she yelled. "You can come out! Hurry!"

Jaye was stumbling along the walkway toward Cara, hobbling a little; at the same time, a blurred mass rose from the mess of broken pipes and slats, through the rushing water. At first it was a large fish, a kind of whiskered, ugly fish with an overlarge head, but before she could even get a good look at the fish it was changing, too fast to follow with her eyes.

And then the fish was her own mother pulling herself up onto the walkway. She was soaking wet, so pale she looked white, and wearing only an oversize, dripping T-shirt that went halfway to her knees. She reached out to hug Cara quick and hard, smiling, water running down her face—and then they were both drenched.

But she didn't look healthy; there were dark circles beneath her eyes, and the lids were red and swollen. Also, she didn't smell so good. In fact, she smelled like something rotten, overlaid with chemicals that had a pungent smell, ammonia, possibly. Cara's nose wrinkled as she pulled away.

"Sorry," said her mother apologetically, still smiling.

Cara realized Jaye was standing next to them, her mouth hanging wide open.

"Hello, Jaye, dear," said Cara's mom. "Forgive my appearance. That water—ugh. It was really getting to me."

"Uh, hi, Mrs. Sykes," said Jaye, and cleared her throat. She looked very confused.

"How are we supposed to get out?" asked Cara. "That—pterosaur? We can't go out the doors. The people are there, the ones with the black eyes."

"We call them hollows," said her mother, and twisted the rope of her long black hair to squeeze out some of the dirty water.

"*Jax's* eyes are like that," said Cara.

Her mother nodded wearily and flicked her arms to shake off water.

"We can't get past them," pressed Cara. "I think that beeping—you hear it?—is some kind of alarm. Isn't it? So how can we get out of here?"

139

Her mother didn't even have shoes on, she saw; she would freeze in the cold October night outside, maybe even cut up the soles of her bare feet…

There was a creak, a heavy, metal creak, and all three of them turned quickly to look. Across the bottom of the tower, one of the big wheel-like things on the insides of the doors was turning, ratchet-ratchet-ratchet.

"It's them!" whispered Jaye, clutching Cara's arm.

"Go," said Cara's mother, and pointed to a door at the other end of the walkway. "I'll hold them off. I was too weak to take any form other than my own; I'll have to build up strength again for that. But the hollows I can probably handle. Meet me where it's safe. Outside the fence."

"How did you—" started Jaye.

"But I don't want to *leave* you," interrupted Cara. "I just found you again!"

"It's the only way, Cara. Your friends need you. The hollows aren't outside the side door now—they're all coming through the front. They're not strategic. More like remote-controlled robots. It could be dangerous for you here. Go!"

Then the far door was swinging open, and backlit by the bright, industrial spotlights outside was a dark crowd of heads and shoulders: the hollows' silhouettes.

Cara and Jaye hesitated briefly, then both turned, ran along the catwalk, and wrestled with the door. For a time Cara didn't see how it opened, but with both of them grabbing and fumbling at the handles and levers they had it open somehow and were outside, standing on the landing of a stairway slatted like a fire escape. Beside them an arc of water sprayed out of the bottom of the tower and was swept away around the base.

If the hollows were dangerous, Cara was thinking, as she stood there uncertainly, hearing the water rush and pour, did that mean Jax was dangerous, too?

"Wait!" she told Jaye, who was clanging down the metal steps ahead of her.

Jaye turned and gazed up.

The door stood open behind them.

Cara felt torn.

"Can't we help her? She's all alone!"

"She said to go, Cara! Didn't you hear? She said it was too dangerous!"

Jaye wanted to go, clearly—she wanted nothing more than to run away. And Cara didn't blame her. But it wasn't her mother back there. What if Cara's mother did need them? What if she *couldn't* handle the hollows?

"And what about Hayley? She's all alone, too!"

"You go," she said to Jaye. "Run to Hayley, OK? I'm coming after you!"

She swiveled and peered around the metal frame of the door.

What her mother was doing now—whatever it was—it didn't look like anything Cara had seen before. She'd seen the wavering, mirage-like ripples in the air that happened when the mindtalkers and mindreaders did their ESP, or whatever it was; she'd seen the threads of light cast over Jax to get the poison out of him.

But she hadn't seen this.

At the far end of the tower, the people called hollows were filing in, ranging themselves along the interior wall. Their movements were unhurried, their gaits slack, but there were more and more of them; they just kept flowing in.

In the middle of the catwalk, between Cara and the hollows, her mother was standing where they'd left her. Her arms were down, her feet slightly apart; she wasn't moving. Some kind of emergency floodlight had come on, dispelling the dimness. So Cara could see that something was happening between her mother and the hollows, and it was happening fast. The network of pipes and wooden slats that made up the floor of the tower was rising, as though pulled up by her mother on invisible ropes—rising to become vertical, as pipes creaked and broke and sections of them fell off, spraying water in plumes all around.

*It's a wall*, thought Cara. *She's building a wall. And it's a wall of water, too, at least for now.*

And also: *My mother can move things without touching them.*

Then, just as the wall reached a height a little ways above her mother's head, the hollows raised their hands above their own heads in a fluid, synchronized motion. Their black eyes grew and grew until the eyes were like saucers; they grew until the eyes joined each other and swallowed up the faces. And then the faces were black holes, and through the holes something was emerging.

It looked like a stream of blackness, a liquid stream expanding in the air; Cara smelled something, something that reminded her of car engines and gas stations. The edges of the stream were orange; the edges were *burning*.

Behind the stream, one of the hollows caught Cara's eye—someone short. A tiny girl with red hair. A girl so little she must barely be out of kindergarten.

But then, beside the little girl—holding onto her hand—was someone else. Cara only saw her face fleetingly—the recognition was so out of place that it took her a second to register it—but the face, she could swear!—the face, with those black eyes in its center, looked like Max's girlfriend. *It looked like Zee.*

And then she had to tear her own eyes away, because the beeping was a scream now, blaring as piercingly as a siren.

"Run, Cara!" cried her mother, who was running along the catwalk toward her. "*Run!*"

They slammed the door behind them, but when Cara turned to lock it, hesitating as Jaye half-dashed, half-limped ahead across the pavement, her mother grabbed her arm and pulled her away.

"It doesn't matter!" she yelled. "The door won't stop it anyway. It'll come out the top. Just run!"

And so they were running, as fast as they could, away from the cooling towers and the shrieking alarm, across the cement to the place where they'd left Hayley.

Looking back, Cara saw the white steam above the tower was turning gray—clouds of gray smoke were puffing up into the center of the white billows, darkening them and making them look ominous. The chill of the night was growing less: around them it was getting warm, and the odor of oil was stronger and uglier in her nostrils.

And then, legs aching and breathing hard, they were around the corner of the first building and there was Hayley, still wearing her absurd pink HELLO KITTY backpack and hugging the book to her chest.

"Mrs.—Mrs. Sykes?" blurted Hayley. "You're practically naked!"

"Out," said Cara's mother, leaning over with her hands braced on her thighs, trying to catch her breath, then gesturing toward the perimeter fence. "Out of the complex. Now!"

Hayley looked blank for a moment, then fumbled with the book, trying to open it, but Cara's mom shook her head.

"That won't work here," she said. "The Burners have the perimeter warded; you have to land or take off from outside the fence. I know you made a call from inside, but you can't travel that way—you can't cross a ward using the windowleaf."

*She must mean the book,* Cara thought, but then they were running again, the three of them following her mother in an exhausted stupor, feet crunching on the dried grass, ignoring the spotlight occasionally sweeping across them, almost blinding them.

Cara worried they wouldn't be able to find the opening in the chain-link again, but just as she felt a needle of despair there it was, the gaping, torn-back triangle of mesh. As they covered the last few steps she realized she was coughing and her throat hurt; the others were coughing, too, laboring hard to breathe. The air was thick with smoke. It was close above their heads; the sky and the stars were completely hidden now, and when she turned around she couldn't even see the massive cooling towers anymore. She couldn't see anything but the bottoms of the buildings, the train tracks stretching out past the flat-topped hills of coal dust, the pavement and the low blanket of smoke. The smog was so dark gray it was nearly black, so thick it looked like it might be solid to the touch.

"As soon as we're through we have to use the book," said her mother hoarsely, and coughed as she crouched down to follow Hayley through the fence gap. "Take us to Jax, Cara."

Cara and Jaye pushed through after her mother, Jaye still hobbling to favor the hurt ankle, Cara holding her hands a little limp.

It was only once they were through—huddling on the dried grass and panting, Hayley still clutching the closed book—that Cara looked down at her mother's bare feet and saw they weren't feet at all. They were large claws.

"Oh, sorry about that," said her mother when she saw Cara staring. "I did it to save my feet from getting torn up, slowing us down. Wait."

All three of them watched in disbelief, breathing hard and coughing, as the claws shrank and formed into bare feet again.

"Let's stay focused," said Cara's mom wearily, and coughed harder. The smoke above them was acrid, its fumes thicker and thicker.

"What's happening?" asked Jaye through a cough.

"It's the Burners," said Cara's mom. "Open the *book*! They're close. We need to go."

"If we go to Jax," asked Cara, "won't they follow us?"

"They can't use the windowleaf," said her mother. "It's only for us."

Hayley opened the book between them.

"We have to hold hands," said Cara. "Or be holding each other somehow, anyway."

"That's right," said her mother. "It has to be done by Cara, but she can't do it alone. Cara, think of Jax. Touch the ring!"

Cara shifted one hand onto the top of the other, palm against the ring, and stared down at the white pages. *Jax, Jax*, she thought. *Wherever you are. Book, take us to my little brother, won't you?*

But the thought was distracted, because her lungs hurt and her nostrils burned whenever she breathed in. She tried to think of Jax and instead kept seeing the black eyes in the face that looked so much like Zee's. Beside her Hayley started to cough harder and harder, and on the other side of the fence forms were emerging from the smoke—the

Burners. She could see the orange glow of their open mouths.

They were moving toward the fence; they were near.

She squeezed her eyes shut for a moment. *Focus, focus,* she told herself. *They can't come with us through the book.*

Her lungs, her throat.

*Don't think of yourself, honey,* said her mother into her mind. *For now, forget our problems here. Think only of Jax.*

The next instant the Burners were through the fence. The mesh was melting at their touch. She wanted to kick herself: she'd forgotten how time flew past whenever she closed her eyes and both hands were in contact with the ring.

She'd lost time, valuable time. Critical time.

"Now, Cara! Now!" Jaye was yelling, and Hayley was on the ground, falling away from Cara in her coughing fit. Cara reached out one arm to make sure she was still touching her, reached out and thought, her whole self moving forward with the urgency of it, *Please, please, take us to Jax!*

She looked up at her mother, who was the closest to the fence, and thought her hair was burning—a red halo around her head. Her mother's hair looked as though it was *on fire.* The Burners were close behind her—almost *on* her—and even as she beheld them and saw the halo of fire, she also felt her mother's eyes on her, steady and unwavering. Her mother didn't seem frightened by the fiery hair, glowing around her head like a nimbus, or the Burners at her back.

Then Cara was stepping into the book, whose white pages had shifted into an image she didn't have time to make out. Without knowing where she was going, she went, Jaye on one side, grabbing Hayley as she moved forward; and this time she made herself trust their future, forced herself to think their fall was a pure, safe arc. She thought of it with a sudden conviction that made her stronger as she felt, again, the sensation of plunging down into a far and empty place.

---

But it wasn't like before.

When they'd come through the windowleaf the first time it had happened fast; this was like slow motion. She could feel her friends' hands on her, their touches at her side and arms, but there was nothing to see. They were floating in a blurred world; nothing was clear. She couldn't see anyone, though the others were touching her sides—Jaye to the left, Hayley to the right—and she could still hear Hayley coughing, though it subsided after a while. She smelled something burnt and bitter.

It was as though they were falling, but falling in a kind of suspended time, almost without velocity.

"Mom?" she called out.

"I'm here," came her mother's voice, in front of her.

"Is—is your hair burning?"

"Not anymore."

"Where are we? What *is* this?" asked Jaye, a little panicked.

"It's OK," said Cara's mother. "We're traveling. Cara, they must be holding your brother in a nether space."

"A *nether* space?" asked Cara.

"Harder to find," said her mother. "Harder to access. You were at the Institute, right, Cara? Remember the elevator doors in the walls?"

"The floors *between* the floors, sort of?"

"The ones marked with the Greek letter $\Psi$. In quantum mechanics they use *Psi* to mean wavefunctions. But the old language uses it to talk about a kind of space that lies between the ones we normally perceive—'nether.' Going to nether spaces takes a while. And whatever you do, keep holding on to each other. *Never let go* in windowleaf travel. People get lost that way. *Badly* lost. Got that?"

"I don't get *any* of this," came Hayley's voice plaintively, and her hand moved a little on Cara's arm.

"Don't let go!" blurted Cara.

"I'm *not*, chick. Think I'm a *total* idiot?"

"It has to do with math, Hayley," said Cara's mom. "How time and space relate. But don't worry, there won't be a pop quiz."

"So why—why were you at that place, Mrs. Sykes?" asked Jaye. "And what happened to their faces? The faces of the hollows?"

So Jaye must have been behind Cara at the door to the cooling tower; she must have been peeking, too.

"The Burners use the hollows as human conduits," explained Cara's mother. "Recently the Cold figured out

149

a way to use the brain's energy as a heat medium for their travel, though it's a slower process than they use with fire. That's how the hollows came to be. Hollows are a doorway for the Burners when they can't make a flame."

The first Burner Cara had seen, on the T, had taken a while to gear up. Maybe because there hadn't been enough heat—unlike with the hotplate in the library....

"Tonight," went on her mother, "the Burners came out of their furnaces through the hollows' bodies. Those furnaces burn at almost three thousand degrees, and that's where the Burners live. Or where they *exist*—I shouldn't call it living. Since they're not alive. The Cold made them in the white-hot furnaces."

"At that place? Where we were?" asked Hayley.

"At power plants all over. Coal-fired plants, natural-gas plants, any place with huge boilers that burn fossil fuels. The Burners don't like the cooling towers because of the wet and cold, but it was convenient, so they had the hollows put me in the tank to force me to shift into a limited, aquatic form. Instant jail. They couldn't keep *me* in the furnaces, after all."

"But why couldn't they just have made you shapeshift into, I don't know, something fireproof?" asked Cara curiously. "And then—"

"I have to take an animal form. I have to preserve my—well, call it a soul. All nature's creatures have souls, no matter what they tell you in school."

"But Mrs. Sykes—I mean, let's say we buy that you can change into animals, since we saw those rad claws," began

150

Hayley. "Still, what about that flying reptile thing? There's extinct animals, there's scary people with black eyes, there are these burning guys…"

"There aren't really extinct animals," said Mrs. Sykes. "Sadly. What still exists are people who can take their *forms*. Some of those people can assume quite ancient shapes—the shapes of creatures that lived here long ago. I'm don't have that range myself. My repertoire's more limited. But the one we call Q for short—short for Quetzalcoatlus, though I think it started as a joke around some TV show—she's older than me. Much. She's…a friend. And a healer. She heard your call and took the form that was needed. It really wasn't the windowleaf that brought her to you—she brought herself."

"It—Q—flew back through the book when you guys were still in the tower. It wouldn't take me there. Maybe it knew you were already coming back," mused Hayley.

"But what do those burning guys *want*?" pressed Jaye.

Around them, the blur was growing more distinct. Lines were gradually emerging, sharper angles.

"The Burners work for the Cold," said her mother. "Like the Pouring Man. Like all the elementals. They do his dirty work. And his dirty work…"

She trailed off.

"What, Mom?" asked Cara.

She was impatient; she wanted to tell her mother about Zee—to ask if there was any way, *any way* at all that the person holding the little, red-haired girl's hand could have *been* Zee.

The pause was dragging on, almost as though her mother wasn't going to answer Jaye's question. But finally she did.

"His dirty work is to remake the world for his own kind. What's happening is a war over that. We call it the Carbon War, but the rest of the world calls it global warming."

They fell silent. Cara's mind raced to a Mars sci-fi movie she and Max had watched a few weeks ago on cable, where people put greenhouses on Mars and tried to make it more like Earth…meanwhile there were colors in front of her eyes, a fuzzy scene whose elements were gradually fading into view. She could see something bright yellow above and below it a row of dots or shapes with a faint blue or purplish tinge, but nothing more specific.

"You're saying global warming is all, like, this cold guy's project?" came Hayley's voice.

"He has allies," said Cara's mom, sounding tired. "Allies who are people. Hundreds of thousands of them. They're helping him make it warmer. Because he wants a different atmosphere, so he can move around freely. Beyond the limited space he's had to hole up in all these years. Once the warming goes runaway—well, then the world will be more his than ours."

"So then there's him and all those on one side, and on the other side there's you, the flying dinosaur, that mermaid from this summer, and some sea turtle in a tank?" asked Hayley. "Is that one a shapeshifter, too?"

"No, a turtle," said Cara's mom.

"And not a mermaid, a *selkie*," said Cara. "Mom, was the *selkie* a shapeshifter? Because if you have to take a form from *nature*—I mean—selkies are from *myths*."

"You'd be surprised, honey. Most myths are more real than you'd think."

And Cara felt her feet connect with solid ground.

## Seven

*The room felt old in the way the core of the Institute had—the* ceilings were high and had fancy trimmings along the edges; the walls were covered in dark wood, and where windows might have been there were old oil paintings, so there was no way to look out—but that wasn't the weirdest thing about it.

What was remarkable was hanging from the ceiling: rows and rows of teardrop-shaped pods, somewhat like chairs she'd seen in sixties décor or futuristic space movies, dangling on thin lines from the high ceiling. Some of them moved very slightly, swaying. Each pod was transparent and contained some liquid, pale-blue in color. When Cara stepped close to the nearest one, she saw the liquid didn't go all the way through; it was in a kind of shell surrounding the interior compartments of the pods.

And inside the pods sat people.

People with black holes for eyes.

"It's a safe house for hollows," said Mrs. Sykes. "We bring them here when we find them, so the Burners can't use them. To protect them until their loved ones can be found—someone who has a memory of them, which can be used to return them to themselves. The earlier the memory, the more completely it captures the person. Cara, my memories of Jax would likely be more extensive than yours—you were only five when he was adopted—so they sent you for me. You see that liquid in the lining of the cocoons? It's a coolant. It keeps the Burners from coming through."

In the pod near Cara an older woman in a white gown sat immobile, looking at nothing out of her deep black eyes.

"Hollows are victims," said her mom. "Some can survive the Burners moving through them once. Some twice. If they're lucky."

Her expression was sad, but she looked healthier now; her strength was coming back. "And now your brother is one of them." She looked around, craning her neck, and they started walking quickly down the row of pods, with Jaye and Hayley close behind. They passed a chubby man with gray beard stubble in denim overalls, a thin little girl... and that reminded Cara.

"Mom? Some of the hollows at that plant were kids," she said, turning around. "And I swear—one of them looked like Max's girlfriend! Zee!"

Her mother looked startled, but before she could say anything a deep voice spoke behind them.

"Lily!"

When Cara's mother saw Mr. Sabin, she smiled: but at the same time she sent something in his direction that Cara couldn't make out. It was like an invisible greeting, a rush of air toward Mr. Sabin from her mother that ruffled what was left of his hair and quickly released it.

Then they hugged normally—though that seemed like an afterthought.

"Glad you're OK," said Mr. Sabin gruffly, stepping back. "Want to see your boy?"

"Take us."

They followed him down the first row and out, past a second row and a third…. Cara couldn't help staring at the hollows in their pods, wondering where the people were who loved them and could help them to get out. They passed a young woman with blue eyeshadow, a tough guy with a shaved head and tattoos of anchors on his arms, a matronly black woman in a yellow pant suit….

"Here," said Mr. Sabin, unnecessarily.

For a long moment they stood there staring at the boy who was almost Jax. He sat in the capsule wearing pajamas that reminded her of a hospital gown, his eyes deep black, his mouth slightly agape as though he'd just seen something surprising. He had a waxlike quality, like a mannequin.

"Oh, man," whispered Jaye. "That's…wow."

"Poor Jax!" said Hayley. "It's like his…personality is gone." She glanced at Cara. "I mean, at the moment."

"His *eyes*," said Jaye.

Cara couldn't say anything at all.

"Ready?" asked Mr. Sabin.

Mrs. Sykes followed him around to the side of the pod, where there was a small hatch in its wall. She stepped up.

"Girls, this is a risky time," said Mr. Sabin under his breath. "If the Burners are paying attention—and they usually are—they get alerted when one of their hollows is exposed. The upside is, your mother, because of her gifts and special connection with Jax, can enact the memory transfer more quickly than many others could."

Suddenly they were surrounded by teachers from the Institute, Mrs. O and others. She hadn't heard them come in. They looked focused on Jax's pod; they didn't speak.

"It's most efficient if she's physically touching him," said Mr. S. "You *must* stay silent. Complete silence is key. This transaction is a work of old language, and it can't be disrupted by any other sounds. OK?"

And then the hatch was open and Cara's mother was reaching in, touching Jax's head with her open hand, murmuring. At once too much was happening for Cara to fathom: there was the now-familiar, mirage-like stream of rippling air between her mother and Jax; there was a hum of sound coming from the teachers, a kind of chant; and there were Jax's eyes.

Which were growing. Just like the hollows' in the tower.

Oh no, thought Cara. This was the Burners trying to get through. It had to be. She grabbed Jaye's arm and squeezed it, wincing at the pain in her hand. On her other side, Hayley grabbed her elbow. Hayley couldn't know exactly what it meant, of course, she hadn't seen what happened earlier, but the sight of Jax's eyes growing larger in his small face was frightening by itself.

*What if it doesn't work?* she thought. *What if?*

Without making a conscious decision, she let go of Jaye's hand with her right one and touched the nazar on her left. *How can I help Jax now?* she asked. *Where is the danger to him here?*

What she saw behind her closed lids was Hayley's pink backpack.

She was so surprised she opened her eyes again, twisting to look at Hayley, who didn't notice because *she* was staring at Jax. Cara could see the pink backpack strap on her shoulder.

What did it mean?

She had to look inside, but she couldn't speak; she caught Hayley's eyes and held her finger to her mouth, moving behind her friend to peel off the pack. Hayley almost blurted something, but Cara shook her head frantically and in a smooth motion had the pack on the floor, its vapidly smiling Kitty staring up at her with a perky red bow in its nonexistent hair. She fumbled to unzip the pack, the rising sound of the teachers' eerie chant in her ears. Hayley bent over beside her as she dumped out the bag's contents in a rush.

There were lip glosses and eyeliners, a blue-and-white tube of pimple cream, a comb and a brush, hair gel, a miniature deodorant, three open packs of gum, nail polish in different bright colors, Hayley's cell phone with its jumble of sparkling stickers…. Hayley was kneeling beside her now, asking mute questions with the expressions on her face. *What's going on?* seemed to be the gist of them, but Cara only shook her head and went on combing through the jumble. It was Hayley's regular stuff, she thought; what could possibly be out of place?

Then Jaye was on the floor with them, too.

Cara had to explain what she was looking for. She grabbed Hayley's phone—would this count as language? She hoped not, she had to get their help—and brought up the notepad function: DANGER IN BAG!

Her friends leaned over, reading the words. There was no disruption in the chant, so Cara guessed texting was OK. Then the three of them were rummaging through the junk. What could it possibly be? This place was supposed to be safe from Burners, Cara thought, so it made sense that the danger had to be in something they'd brought in. The usual safety procedures hadn't been applied to them, she guessed—it had all happened in a rush—

Jaye picked up a plastic bottle: nail-polish remover, that was all. Hayley moved a small pad of paper to grab a metal nail file, which she held up to Cara with an inquiring look. It had a sharp tip, sure—but dangerous to Jax? Cara shook her head.

Then she reached out and took the small bottle of nail-polish remover from Jaye to look at it more closely. In small words the label read INGREDIENTS: ACETONE, DENATONIUM BENZOATE, FRAGRANCE and below: WARNING: FLAMMABLE LIQUID. Something was in the back of her mind, something she couldn't quite recall. It was something a teacher had said—Mr. Sabin, that was it. The words came back slowly. "They can even use flammables—lighters or alcohol...."

*Flammables.*

And just as she remembered that—and hurled the bottle away from her, away from Jax, across the room—the bottle burst into flame.

She wanted to kick herself almost as soon as she did it—she should have doused it in water or something, anything but throw it away. But her *hands*, her hands still hurt with a faint throb, the skin red and sensitive.... She hadn't thought, she'd just panicked. The bottle flamed, it lay beneath one of the pods and flamed—

And they didn't want to call out—they had to stay silent. She whirled around to look at Jax, to look at what was happening right behind her, but as soon as she did she had to look away. His huge saucer eyes were half of his face now, his mouth twisted in a smile that reminded her not of the little boy within or even of the Burners but instead, she realized, of the Pouring Man. It was as though the elementals were all the same, despite their different forms and rules—as though one pure, malicious self occupied all of them. And now that pure malice was taking over her little brother.

Meanwhile the teachers' chant was so loud it was almost deafening, with a pounding, warlike beat—it had changed from soft to loud, almost hysterical... She couldn't stand the sight of her baby brother with that distorted face. She turned her back on it and met the familiar gazes of her friends, who were looking to her for direction: now, this instant, there was a fire burning on the floor, a fire on the floor about ten feet away, and the floor was charring around it, black spreading out from the flames. It hung beneath one of the pods Cara had first noticed: the skinhead with tattoos.

The fire was going to burn him. Not only that—if it spread, all the pods could be ruined and the hollows exposed. Then the Burners could come through and be loose...they were trying to get in however they could, not only through Jax but using the smallest crack, the tiniest item...the battle would be lost.

Before, when her hands got burned, she'd tried to use the rug to smother the flames with; that hadn't worked at all. They needed *water*, and as far as she could see they didn't have any. The only liquid was in the pods, and they couldn't use that.

Water from nowhere, she thought.

She grabbed Hayley's phone and typed on it. NEED WATER!

Jaye was grubbing around in her own backpack, pulling out a bottle; she ran, ducking under the pods in her way; she uncapped her bottle hastily and threw its contents onto the flames.

It had no effect at all. It was just drops, when what was needed was gallons.

Water, thought Cara, which they didn't have.

Or maybe a fire extinguisher. There had to be one, didn't there? Not that this was the kind of place that had modern conveniences, but still. It was supposed to be protected against Burners, so they'd have to have fire equipment; they'd *have* to. She couldn't see from here; the pods were in the way.

So she took off running, between the rows of pods to the wall, away from the fire, from her friends and the crowd around Jax. She ran alongside the big room's wall, passing a glass-fronted cabinet full of what looked like old tools or weapons—the bright-red canister…where was it? There had to be one…then she saw Jaye, at the far end of the room. Grabbing a red canister off the wall.

She felt a surge of gratitude. Jaye had thought the same thing she had; they didn't need ESP for that. She caught up with her friend and they charged back, along the ends of the rows.

But the fire had quickly grown. And it *had* reached the pod containing the big man, the big, shaved-bald man with his tattoos—and as they ran up to the end of the row they saw his pod was collapsed on the floor like a husk and he stood there with flames burning around him—though not touching him—and licking out toward the pods on either side.

And he didn't look friendly as he stood there. He didn't look friendly at all.

Hayley, kneeling a few feet away on the floor, scuttled backwards toward the crowd of teachers, stricken.

Cara turned to Jaye and was about to yell *Now!*—yell it aloud—when she stopped herself just in time; Jaye was already raising the canister and pulling a pin on the top. She aimed the hose part at the floor, the base of the fire instead of the flames; then white foam was spraying out, rising in clouds and obscuring the tattooed hollow man. Jaye swept it back and forth, back and forth.

Off to her right, beyond the clouds of chemical, Cara could see Jax hanging in his pod over the heads of the teachers and her mother, still touching him with her eyes closed. Then the clouds thinned and Cara saw the flames were out; smoke curled from the scorch marks on the floor.

But the big man wasn't standing where he had been.

He had moved. He was standing against the far wall.

Holding Jaye.

He had his hands around Jaye's throat.

Jaye looked terrified. And *he* looked—well, he looked right at Cara.

This was her fault.

Without thinking she ran toward him.

"Let go of her," she cried. "Let go!"

Then she realized she'd spoken aloud, she'd *yelled*—had she wrecked things for Jax? Oh no. But if she had it was too late and now she couldn't stop to look; the big man was shaking his head slowly. He was smiling—that same Pouring Man smile, that knowing smile. He squeezed with his hands, and Jaye made a brief choking noise and then couldn't make any sound at all.

"Stop it!" cried Cara. "Stop! Let go of her!"

She reached out and clutched at his arms, tried to pry them apart, but they were like concrete. Jaye was turning red and tears were streaming from her eyes. Cara grabbed the man's thick fingers next—grabbed at them and tried to pry them backward and off Jaye's throat. She couldn't budge the fingers, either, couldn't even get a firm hold. She was getting desperate.

"Stop *hurting* her! Take *me*!"

And just like that, he let go of Jaye's throat—Jaye fell to the floor, gasping—and reached out for Cara instead.

⚬

The last thing she heard before she left was her mother: her mother calling her name, then the shock of silence.

She didn't leave the usual way; she didn't leave with her body. The big man reached out and in one swift touch made her a hollow. She knew it the moment it happened, knew it with certainty. The way the pen had pricked into Jax's skin, the big man's hand infected her. In that brief touch her mind traveled out of her body.

And just like that she wasn't her whole self: she was a kind of avatar. Unlike Jax she hardly ever played video games, but the few times she'd humored him she'd had a glimpse of something like it—in a flatter and safer version. She was adrift; it was a three-dimensional place, but it didn't seem solid, because she couldn't *feel* it. She saw, but

165

there was no sound or touch or smell or taste, and because this part of her had no lungs or even a heart, there was no rhythm of breathing.

"Jax? Anyone?"

She didn't speak; she only thought of speaking. She had no mouth, after all. It was a shock to realize how hard it was to mark time passing without a heartbeat, the in and out of breath—hard even to *think* right; she had to force herself. It was more like a dream than actual life.

Jax and his friend Kubler liked having avatars because they were little kings in their gaming world, all-powerful—but this was centerless and frightening. She had to make herself remember the people in her life, think *Jax* and think *Kubler*, make herself remember concrete names and things she knew…. It was as though she'd been cut off along her waist, or maybe beneath her neck. She was in a place where no one could find her, where she was utterly alone.

It seemed like a cave, or at least a dark hole shot through with ripples of orange—a formless place whose identity was a mystery. She moved through a tunnel or a liquid; at some remove there were fringes of burning orange and red—tongues of lava pushing through black walls of rock or tar….

For a fleeting second, it occurred to her that if hell were real, a pit of fire like in angry sermons, it might look just like this. And then she recognized something. Out of place in the swirl of darkness with its bright seams, its curves and waves, there was one sharp, *man-made* thing: thin, gray vertical lines or posts: pipes. They were pipes, countless pipes—pipes she'd already seen twice before in visions.

There were pipes rising through the chamber, and as she looked down they disappeared beneath; as she looked up they disappeared above. All she could see was their length and the fact that there were too many of them to count, receding into the distance.

She pushed past them looking for someone—anyone. For information. If only she had a guide, someone to tell her what this was. Did all the hollows experience this? Or was it only another of her visions?

Follow the pipes, she thought.

As she passed them she caught a glimpse of movement up ahead—a white shine in the gloom—and realized it was alive. It was a jellylike, glowing creature that pulsed as it traveled, tentacles rippling. It lit up the dimness, and in its luminescence she saw other creatures, too—creatures she couldn't identify, many of them also giving off light, in various shades and degrees of brightness. Some were crablike, others resembled giant insects, and a few were the red, tube-shaped beings she'd seen in her vision, which looked like a cross between a worm and a tropical flower.

Fear pricked her. She must be in water, because the lit-up creatures moved fluidly. But whether it was a vision or a dream, she wasn't here physically; this wasn't a place where actual people could exist. If it was deep in the sea—assuming this was the place beneath the ocean, the place Jax had talked about, the source—it should be freezing cold, for one thing, or maybe, near the gouts of lava, if that was what they were, boiling hot. But she had a kind of immunity, she told herself: she was only an avatar

She was a figment of her own imagination.

After that she felt less afraid. *Think of it as an adventure.*

She wondered what she looked like to these strange luminescent beings, if they could even see. Some might be eyeless, she thought she remembered from biology.... The pipes must be conveying the gas Jax had talked about, the carbon, funneling it up from who knew where—from somewhere even deeper, deep beneath the earth, up through the water and into the air.

If the minds of all the hollows came here, then it wasn't just her and the deep-sea creatures. There could be someone else—even many others. She thought of the hollows she'd seen in pods in the nether space, tried to call up their faces. Maybe the motherly black lady in the yellow pantsuit was here somewhere, disembodied, or the younger, white woman with the braids and blue eyeshadow, or the thin girl...maybe even Jax.

If he was still a hollow.

Yet if they were here she'd never know: like hers, those other people's minds would be invisible, hovering in the dark.

It might have been minutes that went by or it might have been hours or days. Then something new passed before her. It was like a submarine, lit up from beneath by a carpet of the wormlike forms—curved and flowing and monstrous.

Only after it faded away in the dark did she figure out what it was. She remembered a drawing from one of Jax's encyclopedic books on ocean life.

A squid. A giant squid.

In the wake of the squid a dimly lit school of tiny creatures appeared that flowed past her like a river of light. Whether they were following the squid or just going the same way, she decided to go with them; she simply thought about staying alongside them and there she was, beside the faintly glowing cloud.

Not only her—other creatures were there too, visible on the floor of the ocean and above it, all moving in one direction. Most she didn't have names for: strange, flat fish the color of mud, spiny, many-legged crawlers that reminded her of centipedes, snaggle-toothed fish with lights dangling in front of their faces…. Some made quick, darting movements; others rippled and undulated. There were fearsome-looking things that went past so fast she barely had time to flinch; eel-like fish snaking and twisting along the bottom; more jellies with their tentacles trailing; and translucent organisms shaped like bells and balloons, which she could only make out when something lit was nearby.

She wondered where they were going. Until she realized they weren't going *toward* anything; they were moving *away* from it. They were fleeing—they were in full flight.

Something was chasing them.

She turned her attention backward, against the oncoming stream of strange, deep-ocean life.

At first there were only more creatures, more and more of them moving past, flowing, scrabbling, tumbling over and over each other. Then after waves of them had passed it loomed up: a dark, hulking shape, the thing that was pushing the multitudes out of its way.

It scraped the bottom as it approached, pushing up clouds of debris—sand, rocks, and probably some of the deep-sea life—she couldn't tell, because it churned up the ocean floor and made the water so murky that nothing could be distinguished in the chaos. It had to be some kind of immense vehicle with a wide base like a fan—as though it *meant* to scrape the bottom, as though it was *scouring* the bottom on purpose. A submarine? But submarines didn't move along the ocean floor, did they?

It rose so high she couldn't see to the top; all she could see from within was a dull reddish light. And it took so long to pass that it reminded her of a train, though it was far larger than that.

When it was gone the ocean floor was dark. Devoid of life. Nothing but swirling particles, slowly settling again.

All the living things gone.

She should follow it. Shouldn't she? She could still see its redness, in the distance.

Then something changed and she *couldn't* follow it; she wasn't free anymore. Around her darkness was giving way to a pale, sickly light. She wanted to shy away from it, but she couldn't resist. She heard the pounding of her own heartbeat, duh-*duh*, duh-*duh*. She felt the thin separations of her fingers at the end of her arms, of her feet at the ends of her legs. Around her was a membrane that prickled and tingled and touched against a cold exterior—her skin. It had to be her skin.

She felt her lungs expanding and contracting, and coursing through her was the warmth of blood.

*Eight*

*When she opened her eyes, the first thing she saw was Jax's face.*

It was his *own* face: animated and curious, with standard-issue blue eyes. She felt a rush of relief to see him back to himself—she hadn't ruined things when she called out. At the same time she was so jarred by her own return that she could barely take it in: her head spun. Jax was very close to her, and as she blinked in the light she realized his hands were on the sides of her head.

He took them away and straightened.

"She's back!" he crowed, and turned to the other faces coming into focus behind him: Hayley and Jaye.

Cara's body felt heavy as she struggled to sit up, but the moment passed and she was settled in herself again. The palms of her hands still ached faintly; she'd forgotten about that.

She looked around. She was in an armchair in a small room. She could see a row of pods through an open door.

"I did it!" continued Jax.

Her own Jax. She felt like hugging him, but found she was just grinning dumbly.

"You did!" congratulated Jaye, and clapped him on the back. "Cara! How do you *feel*?"

173

Hayley leaned in close.

"You didn't actually look that bad with black eyes," she mused. "They kind of set off your hair."

"Hayley!" protested Jaye.

Cara remembered, then, the sight of Jaye being throttled by the big man, and felt a start of fear after the fact.

"Jaye—your throat—are you OK?"

Jaye nodded, pulling down her collar to show a couple of bruises on her neck.

"I *am* OK," she said. "Thanks to you."

"That was—that was great what you did, putting out the fire," said Cara, and smiled at her friend.

"Great," said Hayley. "Jaye's the hero. And you're the hero. And Jax is the hero, too. I'm the only one who's not. I messed everything up by having that stuff in my backpack."

"It wasn't your fault, Hay," said Cara.

"Not at all," said Jaye.

Hayley nodded slightly, but she looked distant and a little sad.

"Where's—where's Mom?" asked Cara, stretching out her arms and then rising unsteadily to her feet as her friends and her brother stepped back to give her room. She was conflicted. She was hugely relieved by Jax's return and her own, but part of her—once she got used to it—had almost begun to *like* being bodiless in that deep, dark place, seeing the flashes of mysterious life.

Part of her had grown to savor floating there, after the fear had waned. In the abyss near the source—if that was what it was—and in her avatar state there'd been a thrilling sense of freedom.

"She left with Mr. Sabin and the rest of the teachers," said Jax, his face collapsing into worry. "They—"

"They were fighting the bad guys," interrupted Hayley. "Your mom was like, the leader. She busted out some total martial-arts moves."

"Not *martial arts*," protested Jax.

"It was *too*," said Hayley. "Like in those Chinese movies where they fly through the air. Supernatural kung fu."

"Point being," said Jaye, "she brought down the hollow who had you—and just in time, because it looked like he was going to take off with you somewhere. I mean your body. But then all hell broke loose…."

Cara walked past them to the doorway.

The row of pods she'd seen from her armchair was more or less orderly—except the pods were empty. They were swaying slightly, but on both sides of that one row of pods, the room had been obliterated.

She stood there speechless, staring at the destruction. It was tornado style.

The others came up beside her.

"The whole—the fight to get him away from you? It hit some of the pods, and then before we knew it there were more Burners, coming out of other hollows," said Jaye.

"But the teachers had a protocol for that," said Jax. "These fireproof screens or walls—"

"*Cages*," said Jaye.

"—slid down between the pods and sealed them off into compartments. See?"

Cara could see the crumpled remains of some of these, thin sheets of mesh that were twisted and torn, sticking down from the ceiling and lying jagged in the wreckage on the floor.

"So then there were some hollows raging around in there, like trapped animals, and a couple were still on the loose, you know, with Burners coming through, and Mom and the others—"

"While you were lying there—"

"They had to fight the Burners—"

"We had to carry you," said Hayley. "You were a hollow, too, but Jax was with us by then, he was normal, he climbed out of his pod and the three of us had you and we pulled you in here and Jax did something *amazing*."

"Mom showed me how, is all," said Jax modestly. "She showed me how while she was doing it to *me*. She gave me a model so I was able to stop them from using you—the Burners I mean—as a conduit. And then I brought you back, the way she did with me."

"Your brother," said Hayley, "has serious mental skills. Dude's like a guru. He could have his own *show*."

"But so we were in *here* by then, see?" said Jaye.

"And by the time we weren't totally focused on you, we realized it had gone quiet out there," said Hayley.

"And everyone was gone," said Jaye, and shrugged her shoulders, bewildered. "Just—*gone*."

Cara took it in. She felt sluggish, still half-captured by the deep place and let down to be back in the world only to find her mother had gone away. Again.

"Jax," she said. "I have to tell you something. Mom is— see, she can—"

"Turn into things," finished Jax. "I know."

"It was wild," Hayley told him. "I didn't see her when she was, like, a fish, but I did see these big old claws she had on for a while. Instead of feet."

"Jax," went on Cara, "did you—do you remember what it was like? While you were a hollow?"

"It was like I was just someplace else," said Jax.

"Was it—"

"The source," said Jax. "Or one of them. 'Cause there are more."

"Under the ocean, right?"

"Deep," nodded Jax.

So he had been there, too. She felt a surge of joy: she wasn't alone.

Impulsively she *did* hug him, finally. There would be time later for them to talk about what they'd seen. She looked at him to say so, and he looked back. Even when he wasn't pinging her, they understood each other.

"Aw," said Hayley. "Group hug! No one's a mindless robot anymore. Score!"

The four of them hugged till it felt weird. Which didn't take long.

Hayley pulled back and ruffled Jax's blond hair.

"But there's something I don't get," Cara said to him. "Since Roger's a bad guy—who poisoned you—why did he *tell* Dad, back in August, about the break-in with Mom's computer? About her data being stolen? If it was him who did it, or people working with him, why'd he even *tell* Dad in the first place? Because Dad would never have known otherwise, and *we* wouldn't have known. Right?"

Jax shook his head. "Maybe he figured we were going to find out anyway. Maybe he thought there was a possibility that Mom was in closer touch with us, and he wanted to acknowledge it had happened, sort of to take the blame off himself? Like, pin it on someone else?"

"Could be," said Cara, considering. "I bet he's sneaky enough."

"So anyway," said Jaye. "What's next?"

"Dial up the Marriott!" said Hayley. "Remember? The place we're actually *supposed* to be?"

They didn't know where they were in the world; when they tried to pinpoint their location with the GPS on their phones, they got nothing. It was like their GPSs weren't activated. "It must be that nether-space issue," muttered Jax. "Interesting."

So the easiest way out would be to use the windowleaf. No one knew where it was, though, so they split up and wandered in the wreckage looking for it.

After ten minutes no one had found it, and Cara started to despair. Mysteriously, the big room didn't seem to have exits. The door to the small room with the armchair was the only way out they could see, and *that* room had no *other* doors. It was a dead end.

You could easily feel trapped, she thought, in a room with no doors. As soon as she noticed there were no doors, she started to feel queasy and her pulse quickened.

"It's almost four a.m.!" said Hayley as she and Cara passed in the search. "Good news is, my mom's probably still asleep. Bad news is, if we don't get back before she wakes up, my young, free life is officially over."

Jax found his own clothes in a cubby on the wall and switched them out for the hospital gown he'd been wearing in the pod. He still had no coat, though; Cara made a note to lend him a sweater…. She realized she was yawning, as she wandered in the mess, but despite her fatigue she was growing more and more anxious the longer the book didn't make an appearance.

*No doors*, she kept thinking. *I'm in a room with no doors.*

"Here it is! Here!" called out Jaye.

They ran over, relieved. The book had been hidden by a collapsed pod, which—lying on the floor near a puddle of the blue liquid—looked a lot like a deflated Mylar balloon. The pages were waterlogged at one corner; Cara worried that the book wouldn't work, but she opened it up anyway and bent over the spread white leaves. "You have to hold on to the others," she told Jax, who'd never seen the windowleaf before. They stayed close, their shoulders touching, while Cara put her finger on the nazar.

Just a few minutes later, thinking back, she would realize she hadn't been focused. She was exhausted, and what she thought of when she touched the ring and looked into the book and formulated the words *take us to them* was not the big, bland hotel, where the bus with the purple stripe was parked in the lake-like parking lot and the rest of the team lay sleeping in their rooms. She'd been thinking of that right before she thought *take us to them*.

And then, at precisely the wrong moment, another image flashed into her mind. It was of the hollows from the cooling tower—the one with the face like Zee's, holding the hand of a little girl with red hair.

But one of Cara's friends—she never knew who—was impatient, because before she could even make out the picture that was forming, she was being pulled in. She couldn't let go, because that would be dangerous—if anyone went in without her they could get stranded.

They were going through the opening.

❆

"This is *not* the Marriott," said Hayley.

"Let's go back!" said Jaye. "This—this can't be right!"

They were sitting on a massive concrete platform—a cross between a building and a ship, it seemed to Cara—surrounded by an endless expanse of black ocean far below, with crashing waves. The four of them were squeezed into a small corner of it, where two rails met, behind a hut or a shed or something. Near the edge. It was cold. Looming overhead was a tower and next to it what looked like a crane; stars twinkled in the sky, more than she'd ever seen.

"Just wait," said Jax. "The book's still here. Look. See? So we *can* go back. But let's just take a couple seconds first. To figure out what this is."

"I think it's one of those oil rigs," said Jaye, standing up. "You know, like the one that exploded and killed some people working on it? And all the sea turtles and fish?"

"*Deepwater Horizon*," said Jax, nodding.

Cara and Hayley scrambled up, too, and looked off the rail. They were up high; the platform was tall and massive.

"What's that?" asked Hayley.

Lights from the rig shone onto the water, which shimmered in patches.

"I think it must be oil," said Jax. "Little slicks of oil."

"Spilled oil? Like on that other one?"

"I don't know," said Jax. "But they say there are small leaks and spills a lot, that never get in the news. So maybe…"

He turned to Cara, and she read his expression and nodded. She was getting better at reading him. He wanted permission to ping her.

*What were you thinking of?* came the clear tone of his thought. *What did you think of when you brought us here?*

"The hollows," she said out loud. "And Zee."

"What did you say?" said Hayley.

"We—we must be here because I—see, I saw a hollow, back at the power plant, who looked exactly—"

She almost didn't want to say it, because Hayley bagged enough on Zee already.

"—well, she looked kind of like Zee. She was holding the hand of this little red-haired girl. And just when I was supposed to think of the hotel, I thought of her instead. Of whether it somehow could have *been* Zee. Of that scene. And those two hollows."

"So—whoever the hollow was who looked like Zee, whether it was her or not—this must be where she is now," said Jax. "Otherwise we wouldn't be here."

"Cara, this *sucks*!" said Hayley angrily. "A face *reminded* you of someone, and now we're in the middle of the ocean? I mean Jax is safe, right? Isn't the emergency over? Didn't we win? I want to go back to normal life!"

"Someone *pulled* me through," protested Cara, suddenly feeling angry back. "I *couldn't* let go! It would have been dangerous for you!"

They were startled by a series of loud buzzes, and bright lights shot on—not in the corner where they were huddled, but toward the middle of the rig. The stars seemed to dim overhead.

"What's going on?" whispered Jaye urgently. "Is that for us? Does someone know we're here?"

Jax hesitated, then shook his head.

"I don't think so."

"We need to see what's going on," said Cara. "Please, guys. Because…what if that *was* Zee?"

"Five minutes," said Hayley. "Promise! Until we go back! And I'll hold the book. I'm not letting it out of my sight."

"We can go closer, I think, but just make sure you stay hidden," said Jax.

They crept along the ridged metal wall of the small building. If you leaned against the wall even a bit, it made a cavernous, loud *bong*. Cara jerked her shoulder away.

Peeking around the corner, they saw a clearing in the center of the platform, surrounded by a maze of structures and machinery. It might have been a landing pad, she thought—a helipad?—in any case, a bare paved place with a circle painted on it and then, striking through the circle, some glaring yellow tape in the shape of an X.

And drawing toward that circle with the yellow X were silent people, people shuffling slowly and separately toward the X—trickling toward the middle from all the far edges to converge there. They were all shapes and sizes and ages, from white-haired grandfathers to kids.

Soundless. Waiting.

A kind of awe and chill swept through Cara. It felt sinister.

The crowd on the circle became denser and denser until finally the yellow X had vanished completely. Stadium lights glared overhead, wiping out the sky and the stars, wiping out everything in the wash of their brightness.

*All hollows*, Jax thought at her. *Wait. No, not all. But most of them.*

"Hollows," she heard him whisper behind her to Hayley and Jaye.

*They must be freezing*, thought Cara. Many of the people were wearing nothing but pants and T-shirts, nothing but one layer of cloth against the October cold and the biting wind coming up off the ocean. And yet they weren't shivering, as far as she could see. They weren't doing anything at all.

It made her realize that normally, even when people seemed to be standing still, they didn't really stay still. They did things with their hands—they fiddled constantly, shifted their weight from one foot to the other, messed with their clothes, nodded or coughed—but these people were motionless, from their feet to their hair.

Their bodies were forgotten, she thought—as hers had been, when her mind was underneath.

And then she saw a flash of red hair, low down—and then it disappeared again, behind a dark leg in the crowd.

The little girl. She'd bet on it.

"What are they doing?" whispered Hayley.

"Waiting," whispered Jax back.

Another light flicked on, and partway up the metal tower someone was illuminated. No, several people.

And one of them was Roger.

They were standing on the tower, presiding.

"It's *Roger*," hissed Cara to Jax. "Can you read him? I bet there's tons of secrets in his head that we should know. He's just a regular person, he can't stop you from reading him— can he?"

*Sorry*, thought Jax. *I can't ping him from here, and we can't go closer.*

184

They turned back to the tower, where instead of addressing the crowd Roger was turning to confer with a man beside him. He was wearing a mic, so his voice boomed out over the crowd; but none of the hollows seemed to notice. And in fact, Cara realized, he spoke casually, as though he was in private with a couple of friends.

"OK. Do the partial release," was what he said.

There was a brief electric crackle and then nothing. Or not quite nothing: after a moment, staring into the crowd, Cara saw a kind of domino effect. One hollow would reach out mechanically and touch the next with an arm, and then that one would touch another, and as the arm-touch spread the hollows began to act human again, rustling with slight movement, coughing, sneezing; a couple made short cries or grabbed onto others near them. It was a ripple effect.

Roger waited a bit, till it seemed the whole crowd had been affected, and then raised his arms, palms down, in a calming gesture.

"Some of you are vessels," he said. "And some, sleepers."

Now it *was* like a speech, with a pompous, grandiose tone. Now you could tell Roger had an audience.

*That's what they call hollows*, thought Jax. *The bad guys. Vessel is their word for* hollow. *I can tell because I can read the hollows, and it's part of their lexicon. It's kind of like reading really little kids. They're…infantile.*

"Vessels, you have been brought down to your mundane forms for a short time, to hear me speak, so that your minds can know the task. Sleepers—quietly biding your time until

185

you were called—you are awoken now. Vessels and sleepers, we have gathered you in. For that time has come—the time to join in the great mission. You have been chosen."

There was a murmur in the crowd.

*The hollows can think, on a basic level*, thought Jax, *but they're not free. They're trapped. No free will. But there are others in the crowd I can't read. Those are the sleepers, I guess. It's different from the people at the Institute: I couldn't read them because they knew how to protect themselves from being read. They're adepts. But with the sleepers—I don't know. I'm getting brief readings, and then a kind of static. Trying to read them is like making a call that keeps getting dropped....*

"Each vessel will be paired with a sleeper, to be your guide and your keeper. Each of you has a special task. Each has a target of his own. To realize the dream of the future, you have been called to a duty."

"What is he *talking* about?" whispered Hayley, cranky.

"Out there," said Roger, and gestured with the broad sweep of an arm, "in homes and schools, in office buildings and neighborhoods, there is *dissent*."

Some of the crowd nodded their heads vaguely.

"There is *dissent*, and there are *dissenters*—those who would keep us in this dingy and broken-down old world. Those who fear, rather than embracing, the dazzling prospect of the new. Who cling stubbornly to the old ways."

*Old ways*, thought Jax. *He's talking about us.*

"And some of these dissenters are powerful. A group of them, a small but deeply misguided group, has the ability—and the desire—to stop us in our mission. A mission handed down to us by the One Who Knows."

*That's what they call the Cold*, thought Jax.

"They are spread over the Earth; they lurk in their hidey-holes, waiting to strike. They wear many disguises, but inside they are all the same. They hate us; they hate our perfection. They cower in their filthy nests like creeping things."

A murmur of disapproval went through the crowd. Some people shook their heads.

"And you, my children, his vessels and his sleepers, you have been chosen by the One. Vessels, you have been chosen to stop these dissenters in their tracks. To stop *them* from stopping *us* from doing what have to do. From cleaning up this unclean world, that it may be made new. For we know who these vermin are. And we will root them out. *Sleepers,* sleepers, you will live amongst the vermin. You will pretend to befriend them. You will learn all that you can about the vile dissent. And finally, when the order is given by the One Who Knows, you will deploy your vessel. At that moment, o vessels, you will open yourself wide. You will be channels for the Burners of the One. *And you will incinerate the vermin.*"

His voice dropped, turning raspy.

"You will burn them to cinders."

Behind him a flame sprang up, growing larger and larger. Cara couldn't tell what it was burning on, but the top was blue and there was something hypnotic about its rhythmic wavering.

"In this last war, vessels, your sacrifice will not go unnoticed. Your sacrifice will be the greatest sacrifice of all. And there will be a special place for you in the new world. You will sit at the right hand of the One Who Knows; he will come up on the Earth and reign here forever. You will be kings and queens of the new and everlasting kingdom."

"Seriously?" muttered Cara.

"He's like my uncle Curt, the snake handler!" whispered Hayley.

"*Shh*," said Jax severely.

The tongue of fire was so high now that it almost reached the top of the tower, long and straight and blazing. Cara thought: like a flaming sword.

"Prepare yourselves," said Roger, who didn't seem like Roger at all anymore. "You will be taken to the chosen positions. You will receive your instructions. Now, look there!" And he flung out an arm, pointing dramatically.

All heads turned. Cara heard a whirring sound and saw what looked like a sea of lights in the sky.

Helicopters, she realized. A great fleet approaching.

"Each one of you will be dispatched tonight—each vessel with your sleeper, each pair of you to the place where your sleeper has been dwelling. And there you will take up the duties of your missions."

"We need to be gone by the time the choppers land," whispered Jax. "Or they'll see us. There are too many. We need to go back through the book. *Now*."

"Cara! Let's go!" said Hayley urgently.

The helicopters were closer, almost above them now; the whirring of their blades was loud.

So the four of them squatted down beside the wall of the shed. Just a few feet away the crowd stood entranced, gazing up at the helicopters' lights.

"Don't get distracted this time," said Hayley. "Please!"

"So no one *pull* on me this time!" hissed Cara back. "Wait till I *step*!"

She tried to close out the noise of the choppers and the imprint of the flaming sword—tried to forget the bitter cold numbing her nose and fingertips. She thought carefully of the room in the big hotel, with the painting she'd noticed when they'd dumped their stuff off and left for the meet. It was practically the only thing she *did* remember about the room, so she focused on it: a man in a red coat and black helmet sitting atop a brown horse. It hung over one of the two beds. Behind the horseman was a landscape she guessed was English, with rolling green hills and hedges. She thought of that scene and realized she could remember the bed beneath, with its homely maroon bedspread of flowers and paisley.

Details, details—she had to fix the details in her mind. *Take us.*

And there it was, surfacing across the fading pages of the book: their hotel room, in all its boringness. The red-coated man on the horse (which looked like a Paint-by-Numbers). There was the bedside table with an old TV remote and a phone.

"Go," said Cara, and stepped forward.

But as she stepped, she raised her eyes and caught sight of the very edge of the crowd, which was spreading out again as people retreated from the helipad to make room for the descending helicopters. The rotor noise was deafening, and wind was blowing people's hair around. And on the edge of the crowd, just as it vanished from her sight, she caught sight of a flash of red hair and, not far above it, one more time, the face of Zee.

⚌

They landed next to the hotel bed, with Jax sliding down the side of it and onto the floor, snagging a coverlet with his foot.

Cara had never felt so relieved to be in a hotel room. The stale warmth of the wall heater washed over her, making her frozen fingers and burnt hands feel better right away, and the tacky décor was comforting.

They sat there a minute, relaxing as they adjusted. The book had fallen on the floor, too, the nubbly brown carpet beside Jax. Cara took in the cabinet with the TV in it, the brochures on the table, the chunky lamps. The clock-radio on the nightstand read 4:44. She was too tired to think of Zee's face, of any faces at all. All she wanted in front of her eyes was her pillow.

Jaye released her breath in a sigh.

"Oh my *God*," she said. "Is this really the normal world again?"

But without waiting for an answer, she climbed onto the bed and under the covers. She closed her eyes.

"I'm wiped," murmured Hayley.

Cara moved onto the other bed, though it was hard to move at all; her body just wanted to stay put. They were all collapsing without even changing into their pajamas—Cara and Jax in the second bed, Hayley tucked in next to Jaye on the first. There was a bedside lamp on, but Cara was too tired to get up and turn it off.

## Nine

*It seemed like only moments later that Cara heard the sound* of the lock on their door clicking, and before she could even move the door opened.

There was Hayley's mom in all her big-hair glory, sporting a hot-pink jumpsuit that made her look like some kind of high-fashion paratrooper.

Cara rubbed her eyes and sat up in bed. Morning light leaked in along the edges of the heavy hotel drapes.

"Rise and shine, girls!" said Mrs. M brightly, and then saw Cara. "Cara! *Jackson!* Well, I'm glad you're feeling better, Jax. I'm glad to see the staff at the Institute brought you two back last night instead of this morning. Though of *course*—this goes without *saying*, Cara—you should have checked in with me the very *minute* you arrived!"

"I'm really sorry, Mrs. M," murmured Cara.

"It's only because your father trusts those people so much, and the lady on the phone seemed so on top of things, that I didn't have a *coronary*. But that doesn't change the fact that you snuck off behind my back, and we'll have to have a little *talk* later about your *escapade*. And with your daddy, too. What you did is serious, girl. You could have been real badly hurt. Or lost. Heaven *knows* what."

She shot Cara a stern look, the kind that promised a future campaign to convince Cara's dad to ground her. Cara nodded, penitent. Mrs. M, who Cara suspected didn't like to be tough but felt she had to, cleared her throat then and reached up to fiddle with one of the beads on her necklace.

Despite the stern look, Cara felt she was getting off easy—way easier than Hayley would if her mom found out what *she* had done.

"Anyhow, it's a relief you two are back," said Mrs. M, in a more normal tone. "I worried that if they waited to drop you off at the meet, Cara might miss her race. Of course, your older brother's girlfriend has *also* gone off-campus, Cara, as you may have heard. Quite a handful, that one, is what *I* hear. We're still working on it."

She strode over and tugged on Hayley's blankets.

"Come on. Up and at 'em, little mermaids!"

"Mom, please," groaned Hayley. "I'm not even *competing* today. And Jaye's an alternate. Why can't we just hang here and sleep in?"

"This is a *team* effort, Hayley. You're not going to abandon the team just because you stayed up late chit-chatting. Now up! The continental breakfast is almost over. They have those Danishes you like. Cherry!"

Hayley groaned again, and Jaye pulled the coverlet up closer to her chin.

It struck Cara that Mrs. M shouldn't see that Hayley and Jaye had gone to bed in their street clothes—which were dirty, torn, and probably smelled like smoke. So she threw back her own blankets and moved to get up, to try to keep Hayley's mom's attention on herself.

But touching the covers made her palms smart, and she jerked them back again.

"My *Lord*, what happened to your hands?" burst out Mrs. M, apparently not noticing her clothes.

"Oh," said Cara. There again, she hadn't thought up a story yet.

"It was so hot…," began Hayley

Cara glanced at her, alarmed.

"It was so hot in here. We couldn't sleep," she went on, sounding more sure of herself. "From the heater—that one. On the wall under the window? So she got up in the middle of the night to turn it down, but it was dark, and I guess the metal on that thing gets really hot."

"My Lord!" said Mrs. M again, and bent down to touch Cara's wrists delicately, turning them so that her hands were palms up. "That's criminal! That's just negligent! And a fire hazard, too! My goodness, you poor thing! We should sue the pants off them!"

"No, it's OK," said Cara. "It's not that bad. Really. We iced it. Hayley and Jaye helped me. With—er, ice from the ice machine."

Fleetingly, she was proud of herself for coming up with that.

"But how will you *swim*?" asked Mrs. M, indignant. "You can't swim with those hands! There's no way," and she shook her head. "I can't allow it. Your father would have my head on a platter. Nosirree. Nuh-uh. Jaye, honeypie, this is your lucky day. You're going to sub in for Cara on the relay team. And Cara, I'll get you some medicated lotion at the CVS or what have you. There's one next door. You will sit tight today with your hands wrapped or my name is not Delilah Moore."

"I didn't know your name was Delilah," piped up Jax. "Like with Samson!"

"Yes, dear. Well, now you do," said Mrs. M, and groped around in her handbag till she found her cell phone, which she flipped open. "Old Testament names were very popular in my neck of the woods. I mean it, Cara. No way are you swimming with those hands. I'm sorry to disappoint you, but that's the way it's got to be."

In fact, Cara was relieved. At the moment she felt way too exhausted to swim. She shot a look at Jaye, still wearing covers up to her neck, and could tell she wasn't psyched to be taking Cara's place.

"Girls, get dressed while I talk to Coach about this injury situation. Come on. Jackson, you too. You stay close to me today. I want to be able to tell your daddy I took good care of you. Don't dawdle, Hayley. And brush your teeth, everyone. No morning breath on my watch! I'll step into the hallway right here and make a call or two. Y'all be ready to go down for Danishes in five."

As it turned out, Hayley took fifteen minutes to get dressed, or five to get dressed and ten to apply lip gloss and eyeliner and do her hair, and they completely missed the free breakfast, which irritated Cara since she was starving. As they surged through the hotel lobby to get on the bus, they converged with the rest of the team, who were talking and joking loudly, their knapsacks slung over their shoulders. She'd given Jaye the windowleaf to store in her big duffel—the only bag they had that the book would fit inside—and Jaye was carrying the bag awkwardly, bouncing at her hip.

At the meet Cara, Jax, and Hayley headed for the bleachers with Mrs. M while Jaye went off with the rest of the girls to change in the locker rooms. Mrs. M didn't waste time; she made Cara hold out her hands and smoothed on some medical-smelling cream. She was so good at it that she seemed to Cara less like a hairdresser than a nurse. And right away her hands felt so much better that Cara was surprised.

The gun went off for the first relay heat, and swimmers hit the water. Cara's cell rang—it was Max calling; she knew from the ringtone—and Jax answered because she couldn't, with her hands slathered in greasy lotion. Mrs. M was sitting right beside them, so Jax couldn't tell Max what had really happened; Cara had to listen to him giving Max the made-up homesickness story. Just as their school's team, including Jaye, assembled behind the starting block for their heat, Jax changed the subject.

"Hey. But with Zee," said Jax, and met Cara's eyes. "You know she left the meet, right? I mean, she's going to be in trouble. Um, do *you* know where she is?"

Mrs. M turned and looked at him, waiting for Max's answer, but after a moment Jax shrugged and shook his head, like Max wasn't saying anything important.

"Why don't you just *text* Max?" said Cara, and nudged Jax's foot with the side of her own. "It's so *loud* in here."

"Oh yeah," he said, and hung up.

The heat was ending—it looked like the team wasn't out in front, so Cara stopped paying close attention, but the other teams vying for first and second place cheered louder. When the swimmers touched the wall, their team had placed fourth, which meant they hadn't made the final. The cheers trailed off, and the last swimmer hauled herself out of the pool; she and Jaye, who stood dripping nearby with red circles from her goggles around her eyes, shook their heads ruefully as they slipped off their swimming caps.

"I think," said Mrs. M suddenly, pronouncing it *Ah thank* as usual, "that since none of you have any more races—and since we have Jackson to get home and your hands are injured, Cara—that we should go ahead and take the ferry back this afternoon. We can swing by the hotel first to pick up our things. There are plenty of chaperones; Mr. Abboud has already taken over the other kids on my list. So we'll just scoot to the ferry dock on the T. It goes right there. And I bet your daddy can pick us up in P-town. We can squeeze into y'all's Subi if someone sits in the way-back. OK?"

"That'd be good," said Jax, nodding.

*At home we'll have more room to breathe*, he thought at Cara. *We need some privacy. I texted part of it to Max but not all and so he's kind of freaking out.*

"Exactly, privacy," she blurted out.

"What's that, sweetie?" asked Mrs. M.

"Oh, nothing. That sounds great, going home early."

Although she had to admit, her hands felt so much better it was almost as though they hadn't been burned in the first place.

"What *was* that lotion, Mrs. M?" she asked. "It made my hands feel completely better."

"Just cooling gel!" said Mrs. M, and turned away to beckon to Hayley, whose attention she was having trouble attracting. She stood up on the bleacher to wave her over.

Hayley wouldn't be happy about leaving Boston early, Cara realized. Jaye would; there was a rehearsal for the school play tonight, which she'd complained about having to miss in order to make the trip. Now she wouldn't have to miss it. But Hayley would be mad; she'd been looking forward to tonight, when the team was scheduled to have a social hour in the hotel restaurant with the teams from the other schools. Hayley lived for things like that.

"Should I break it to her?" Cara asked Mrs. M. "Or should you?"

⊰⊱

199

Sure enough, Hayley sulked on the ferry. While the others went out on deck, she sat hunched up with a shut-down frown, texting rapidly on her phone.

With Jax on one side and Jaye on the other, Cara stood at the rail and smelled the salty spray.

"So?" asked Cara. "What did Max tell you about Zee?"

"He didn't know anything," said Jax. "He sounded pretty worried."

"It really looked like her!" burst out Cara. "I saw her again when we were stepping into the book, off that oil rig—I could have sworn it was her. Seriously."

"So we think Zee is mixed up in all this, too?" asked Jaye.

"It has to be because of us," said Jax solemnly.

"Like they could have taken her because she knew us, you mean? Like, say she's a hollow. Like you were. And I was, too. So then, maybe they picked her because she knows us. Maybe *you're* the target they want to aim her at! Or Mom is!" said Cara.

"I guess that wouldn't be such a stretch," said Jax. "If it really *was* Zee you saw…."

"We have to find out," said Cara. "We have to go and get her! And bring her out of it, like you brought me. Right? You stopped me from being a hollow—you brought me back. If we could find her, you could you do that to her, too, right?"

"But I don't *know* her that well," he said. "I *know* you. It works through accessing a *memory*. Remember?"

"But you do *know* her," said Cara, though she felt uncertain.

When they'd sent her to find her mother, the teachers at the Institute had assumed that even Cara's memory of Jax, her little brother, wouldn't be enough. So what were the chances her or Jax's memories of *Zee* would be?

They all stared off the rail at the gray ocean. The mainland was too far behind to see anymore.

"Is that the only way to help them?" asked Jaye, after a minute. "The memory thing?"

"It's the official way the dissenters have," said Jax, thoughtful. "For curing the hollows. I mean the hollows have only existed for a few years. Most of the dissenters' methods are *way* older than that. I don't even *know* how old. But my point is, they may not have figured out the best way to fight the hollows yet. So…maybe I could try something else. It's possible. But it could be risky."

"What could you try?"

"I think maybe I could *go* there. Go to where they are. The Rift Valley. The Rift Valley of the Mid-Atlantic Ridge."

"Go there?" echoed Jaye.

Her nose was red and running in the cold wind off the water, Cara noticed, but she wasn't complaining.

Unlike Hayley, who was warm and comfortable inside the boat and in a worse mood than anyone. Because of Cara, she and Jaye had both had to go through this—but in fact, she'd had a way easier time of it than Jaye. No one had tried to strangle *her*.

Still, here was Jaye, cheerful and friendly, and there was Hayley, the prima donna.

"With my mind, I mean," explained Jax. "And if she's there, I think I could find Zee's mind, too, in with the other hollows. Because when I was a hollow and went there, I could read them all around me."

"I wondered about that," said Cara, and felt almost sad. Unlike Jax, she'd been alone.

"I think any hollow in our neck of the woods would be at that source, instead of one farther away. Just like we were. The Cold is systematic. And maybe, if I had someone to help pull me back…. We'd have to be in the same place, Zee and I. So I mean, first we'd have to find her physically. And then, assuming she was a hollow, we'd have to get her in a room and someone would have to guard us, her and my body, while I was out basically, you know…looking for the rest of her."

Jaye shook her head, half disbelieving.

"Say it didn't work," said Cara. "What could go wrong? Could you get hurt?"

They *should* take a risk to get Zee back. Because what had Roger said? If she *was* a hollow, she was just waiting to be a so-called channel for the Burners' fire, or something. She was in danger right this minute. And always, from here on out.

But what about Jax—should they really risk him again? She couldn't forget those black eyes, expanding in his face like pools of spilled liquid. It made her scalp creep thinking of it; she could hardly believe it had been just hours ago.

"I think the worst-case scenario would be failing— that I couldn't get her back. I don't think they can make me a hollow again. Or you. If you get pulled back before the Burners use you, I'm pretty sure you're immune. The Burners use this one connection in the brain, this one pathway, that kind of gets destroyed in the process. Like a short circuit, basically. So they can't use it to get in again."

"But *they* brought the hollows back, didn't they? Roger and them? When we were on the oil rig? *They* brought them back to consciousness so they could give them their instructions. Remember?"

"Not really. It's like hypnosis, where there are different levels of sleep—they can bring the hollows up from the deepest level, where they have those black eyes and are open for the Burners, without waking them up all the way. When they're in lighter states, they don't have the black eyes; I think they might look like regular people. They're practically robots when their eyes are like that, they only understand basic commands. Nothing complex."

"We should talk to Max," said Cara. "Let's ask him what he thinks as soon as we get home. Let's ask him if he'll help us look for Zee."

"Kids?" called Mrs. M, standing at the door to the ferry's cabin. "Come back inside! You'll catch pneumonia out there for so long!"

They followed her back in, holding on to posts and the backs of benches as they walked down the aisle and the boat bucked and dipped. When they got to their row of seats, Jaye sat down next to Hayley and nudged her softly.

"What's so urgent you have to go all sixty-words-a-minute on us, Hay?" she asked.

"Maybe I had a chance to actually *bond* with people, and now it's totally wrecked. And maybe standing out there with you guys, getting drenched by polluted water and freezing to death's not my idea of fun."

"Don't be rude, Hayley," chided Mrs. M. "You're not a holy martyr suffering on a cross. You're just a girl who had to leave her swim meet a weency bit early."

"You don't know *anything*," said Hayley churlishly, half under her breath.

"Oh no?" asked Mrs. M. "Well, you should feel free as a *bird* to share with me."

Hayley shot Cara a dark look. Cara knew that look: this was one of Hayley's moods. Now that the excitement was over, she was blaming Cara for ruining her social plans. Hayley had many social plans. Some were so minute they were invisible to the untrained eye. But she was always planning.

Cara tried not to feel irritated by Hayley. Back in August, true, her oldest friend had asked to be included; but now school was on and she wanted to do regular things. She hadn't asked to be chased by cloned, inhuman-seeming men, to put out fires or watch one of her best friends get burned and the other get throttled.

*Her* mother wasn't missing, after all.

Cara wondered what her own mother was up to. What, and where, and whether she was still fighting. (Hayley had said, with admiration, *supernatural kung fu....*)

She should be more generous. Hayley was basically an innocent bystander in all this.

"I'm sorry, Hay," she said softly. "I'm sorry I messed up the trip for you."

"Nonsense," said Mrs. M stoutly. "You did do wrong to run off without permission, I admit that, but us going home early isn't your fault. We have Jackson to return, and your hands—well, that was purely an accident."

"I'm sorry anyway," she said, and tried to catch Hayley's eye. Hayley knew what she meant, even if Mrs. M couldn't.

"Me, too," Jax said.

But Hayley wouldn't look at either of them, just gave an angry toss of her head and went back to her texting.

Mrs. M brought their dad up to speed on the official version of events from the passenger seat in the Subaru. Heading home from the ferry dock in Provincetown, Cara, Jax, and Jaye sat in the backseat and Hayley curled up with their bags in what her mom called the "way-back," self-isolating with her phone.

"I apologize for not calling you right when this happened, William," said Mrs. M. "But just a few minutes after I realized Cara was gone, when I was still brainstorming what to do, the nice lady at the Advancement Institute called. She'd gotten my number from Cara, and she told me the kids were doing fine, with details right down to what Cara was going to be having for dinner. She was very reassuring. So I decided not to bother you."

"All's well that ends well, I guess," said Cara's dad. "But Jackson, you should have let me know you were homesick. I would have driven in and picked you up myself."

"I just got scared, all of a sudden," said Jax. "And Cara was near. That's all."

"Of course, William, I'm sure you'll want to have a serious talk with Cara about what happened here," said Mrs. M. "The risk she took. I *did* express my deep *disappointment* at her irresponsible behavior, both as her chaperone and as a family friend. It goes without saying she should have contacted you about Jackson and stayed where she belonged. I shudder to think what could have happened there. But the discipline is your area."

"I certainly will have a talk with her," said Cara's dad, and caught Cara's eyes in the rearview mirror, glowering. "I certainly will."

All things considered, though, the talk wasn't too harsh. Cara's dad had never been too comfortable punishing the kids; the worst thing he ever did was give them extra chores or, if he was feeling like he really had to make a show of it, saying they couldn't watch TV. In this case, he opted for telling Cara she had to help Lolly keep the house cleaner—and, of course, that if something like this ever happened again, etc.

He cleared his throat awkwardly at the end of that speech, then patted her on the shoulder and retired to his office to do more writing about the back-whipping guys.

Cara grabbed a couple of slices of cinnamon-swirl bread from a bag on the kitchen counter—she was ravenous—and then took the stairs two at a time up to Jax's room, tearing off generous bites of the soft bread as she went. It was just the two of them and their dad in the house at the moment; Lolly didn't come over till just before dinnertime on weekdays. Since it was afternoon, Max was still in classes, although the school day would end soon.

On Jax's door Messy-Hair Einstein hung droopily, attached by a single piece of tape. She reached up and restuck the other piece of tape on top of the poster with a fingertip, then knocked as she turned the knob.

For a second, stepping into Jax's domain, she missed the days when she'd had to watch out for slugs and crabs crawling around. Now there were elaborate Lego machines underfoot, plus stray bright-colored blocks whose corners were surprisingly sharp when you stepped on them.

Jax was kneeling on his rug, halfway under his desk, setting up his backup computer—a.k.a. *her* computer—by plugging various cables into a power strip on the floor. His own laptop, of course, had been abandoned in his room at the Institute, along with his phone.

When they got the windowleaf back from Jaye—Cara had forgotten to ask for it when they dropped Jaye off— they could maybe get his tech back faster that way, she thought.

"What did Dad say?" he asked from beneath the desk, his voice muffled.

Cara sat down on the edge of his bed, though a chair would have been better. Among the messed-up covers were books, a greasy plate, a stray fork, and what appeared to be a large horseshoe magnet (which the tines of the dirty fork stuck to). She picked up the magnet/fork combo and placed it gingerly on a shelf.

"Extra chores," she reported. "Other than that, he let me off with a warning."

Jax scooted out from under the desk and straightened, dust bunnies hanging from the knees of his jeans; he hit a key on the laptop to boot it up, then sat down hard on his swiveling desk stool, which made a quick wheeze.

Suddenly he froze, then blinked and shook his head, as if to clear cobwebs.

"They have this place warded," he said abruptly. "The whole block, down to the water. I just *got* it. Just now. The opposite of sensing danger. A kind of security fence, you know? I can feel the lines of it, the way you'd see laser beams crossing each other in a movie about a museum robbery. Warded, like with the charm we did in August, to make the house safe for Mom to come back?"

"There were wards at the power plant, too—where we found Mom. So now you're sensing them?"

"I learned a lot down in the Rift Valley."

"Did you see the animals, too—the glowing deep-sea animals? And was there lava where you were?"

Jax nodded. "And then there was the infrastructure of the Cold."

"The pipes?"

"He pumps the gas from deep down, I think. I mean I don't know the mechanics of the process. I didn't even know there *were* major reservoirs of $CO_2$ in the mantle before this. I thought it was just shifting rock and sometimes some magma or whatever. Geology's not my best field. But I guess there must be. Because he definitely brings it up from somewhere. And he delivers it through the pipes."

"Did you also see the machine? The machine scraping the bottom?"

Jax looked surprised.

"No."

"It was some kind of huge vehicle. It scraped the bottom of the sea. I think it must have killed everything in its path. But that was all I could see; it passed me, and it was chasing all these animals in front of it. And then it was gone."

"It must be a part of his—what does he call it? His 'Cleaning Initiative.' One of the three prongs."

"Prongs? How did you *learn* all this?"

"I did get readings off some of the animals in the Valley, but the readings were hard to understand—our brains are too different. Well, they mostly don't *have* brains is the thing; they have these spread-out nervous systems…starfish, for instance. Sponges don't have centralized brains *or* nervous systems. Sponges aren't rocket scientists."

"No kidding."

"I could read the sea turtle last summer, remember? It had this deep intelligence. But sponges? Forget it."

"So where'd you—"

"Mom. When she pulled me back it was sort of—through her mind. And I picked up all this data, just lying around in there."

He grinned his little-boy grin.

Cara gaped at him, then realized she looked idiotic and shut her mouth.

"So the main prong is global warming, which he calls Atmosphere Adjustment. He likes these official-sounding names. Then there's what scientists call ocean acidification, which he calls Marine Modification. The third prong is the Cleaning part. He wants to get rid of a long list of life forms, like most of them, to make room for his favorites. A few he's going to help survive to be resources in the new world. Like, in the oceans I think he likes jellyfish. Actually that's a misnomer, they're not true fish at all. Some of them are allied with him, and algae, I think, but I can't keep them straight, the algaes and plankton, some are with us and some with him. Technically even jellies are plankton, a kind of megaplankton also called gelatinous zooplankton, but then you also have your macroplankton—ctenophores, salps, doliolids, and pyrosomes—"

"*Jax!* Down, boy!"

"But coral reefs? Forget it. Reefs are his enemies. They're all on our side, all of them. Every single reef species. Not only the corals but all the colorful reef fish like you see in aquariums—they're already dying off around the world because of carbon. And cetaceans. We have *all* the dolphins, *all* the whales…and the mollusks. Every shell-forming organism in the ocean is on our side."

"And you got this from Mom's brain?"

"Well, her mind. It's not *equivalent* to her brain. But close enough."

"Um."

"And on land it's mostly the weedy species that are with him—things that survive in garbage dumps. Although there was a suggestion that the ants could be his. Like, *all* of them. If that's true, it'd be bad. Because ants? There are a *lot*. Some scientists think they may make up a *quarter* of the total biomass of all land animals."

He got up from his chair and pulled open his window; a rush of cold air made Cara shudder.

"What'd you do that for? You're letting the heat out!"

"Shouldn't we want to stay cool, anyway? With all those Burners gunning for us?"

"But you said our block was warded."

"Yeah. I'm kidding. Mostly."

He leaned down and stared at a seam on the wooden window frame.

"What are you *doing*?" she asked.

"Looking for them. The ants. I just remembered that all summer, whenever I opened this, there was this line of red ants along the window sill. Right here."

He pointed, then shrugged.

211

"Of course, they're all gone now. Anyway. It's not like they would do anything, individually. They're still ants. But if you got enough of them…"

"So—wait," said Cara, and he pushed the window down again. "When Mom gave us that message for Dad, was that what she was talking about? *The animals aren't what they seem.* She told me it was a line they both knew; she said it was mostly meant to let Dad know we'd really been in touch with her. Like, proof. But if the line about that—that some animals are on the other side, though most of them are with us—does that mean Dad *does* know about some of this? About the Carbon War?"

"I can read him, if you want. We'd just have to figure out the right question to ask."

The conversation she'd had with her mother while they traveled to the nether space—about how the Cold was an alien, how he and his allies were responsible for global warming—had faded in her memory, as though a gauzy film had been thrown over the parts that weren't the most dramatic. She struggled to bring back the details. About the animals, what had her mother said, exactly? She'd said the sea turtle was really a sea turtle, but the flying beast that seemed like an extinct Quetzalcoatlus wasn't actually one….

"She did say there are animals *and* shapeshifters on our side," she said. "And that the flying dinosaur thing is one of the shapeshifters. It's a she, I guess, and they call her Q."

"Not flying dinosaur," corrected Jax. "Just *pterosaur. Azhdarchidae*: advanced, toothless—"

"But my point is, she *isn't* that," broke in Cara. "Mom said that shapeshifters—like her—well, some of them can take ancient forms. That's what Q does. Mom can only take the forms of things that exist now, I guess. So she was the sea otter. And when they threw her into the basin beneath the cooling tower, she turned into a fish."

"So there are human shapeshifters and ones that aren't human, I guess," said Jax. "I mean, in their first forms."

Her mother had said that, too: "first form." *If I were in my first form....*

"But, um," said Cara, "Mom's *first* form is human. Right?"

"I think so," said Jax. "But..."

"But what?"

"Well, it's obvious. But if she's human, then some humans are shapeshifters, which implies..."

He trailed off again.

"*What*, Jax?"

"That human doesn't really mean what everyone thinks it does."

A few minutes later, both of them still hungry from missing breakfast and lunch and hardly sleeping the night before, they went down to the kitchen to forage. Cara stuck her head in their father's study door to say hi, then closed the door when she withdrew. She and Jax were standing in the kitchen eating the rest of the cinnamon-swirl loaf, slathered with butter, when Max's voice rang out behind them.

"Homes!"

They turned and looked down the front hallway as their older brother dropped his backpack on the floor and plucked his earphones out of his ears.

"Good to have you back, small man. Cara. So what's the 411 on Zee? You find out anything more for me?"

Jax glanced at Cara.

"Long story," she said.

## Ten

*They told Max everything—ending with Cara thinking she* saw Zee. The three of them crowded into Jax's room, scarfing pretzels and talking fast.

"I can't believe this," said Max, crumpling the bag and lobbing it into the already-full trashcan beside Jax's desk. (It bounced off and hit the floor.) "It *can't* be her. I can't believe someone actually messed her up in this. I didn't even *tell* her about the summer. I didn't want to freak her out. Are you sure? You could have imagined it. Right? *Easily.*"

"I know," said Cara. "I could have. But shouldn't we find out for sure?"

"You're saying you can take this book—this book that lets you go wherever you want to—and use it to find Zee? Just by thinking of her?"

"Well," said Cara. "I hope so. I don't know for sure. When we used it before, I had to have Jaye *and* Hayley to make it work. Because they're both...so close to me, I guess. You can't use the windowleaf alone; you need your friends for it to work right. A circle of them. Now Hayley's mad at me. But if you and Jax take her place— maybe."

"And if we do find her, Jax plans to do some ESP thing to get her head on straight again? If she *is* messed up by these…Cold Ones?"

"There's only one Cold One," corrected Jax.

"I guess so. Basically," nodded Cara.

"But that would be just a big experiment, with Zee as the guinea pig! Jax, you *admitted* you don't have a clue what you're doing. It'd be a total shot in the dark!"

"But Max," said Jax, "if she *is* a hollow, and the other option is leaving her that way…you don't want that for her. I promise."

"Listen. If we do find her, and there's something messed up about her eyes—which, by the way, I'm not saying I believe there's gonna be—then no offense, kid, but I'd want to call Mom in on that. I'd want to leave it up to the professionals."

Jax looked downcast. The confidence he'd shown just instants before Max got home seemed to shrink, which made him seem younger.

"Easier said than done," said Cara. "Calling in Mom, I mean."

"I tell you what," said Max. "Cara, if you get that book back from Jaye, then I'll go along with you. We'll leave Jax here, since he's a target. Inside the so-called wards. He'll be safe, right? And you and I can take our chances and see if that window thing can bring us to Zee. Because other than these stories you guys are telling me, I got nothing. And, yeah, she cuts class sometimes, but when she does it's usually with me. So this is weird. But if we find her, and if there is something seriously wrong, like, physically, all I'm saying, I'm not going to rely on a little dude to fix it."

"Jax's instincts are better than you give him credit for," said Cara, defensive. "Better than mine, anyway. *Or* yours."

"Except only yesterday he was taken over by aliens and had to be locked up in some kind of futuristic pod deal, am I right? So he doesn't exactly keep himself safe 24-7. Does he."

"That was *my* fault," said Cara. "*I* handed him the poison pen. Or whatever you want to call it."

Jax shook his head.

"Max is right," he mumbled, and picked pieces off a Lego crane, not meeting her eyes. "It was my fault. I was distracted, and I messed up."

"Listen," said Max, and elbowed Jax softly. "I didn't mean to run you down. But you're ten years old, Jax. Even if my whole brain *would* fit in your frontal lobe. And if Zee's— if something's happened to her...I mean this summer, *I* screwed up. I got the car totaled because I wasn't taking stuff seriously, and I left you guys on your own. I still feel guilty. I don't want to make a mistake like that again."

They sat there in a silence that wasn't so bad. It was comforting to hear Max say he felt—well, anything.

❦

An hour later Jaye's mother stopped the car outside the Sykes's house on their way to Jaye's play rehearsal. Jaye had told her the windowleaf was an atlas from the school library that Cara needed for homework, so Mrs. Galt talked away on her headset, paying no attention to the girls as she idled in front of the lawn and Jaye and Cara met halfway up the walkway, Jaye clutching the book.

It was chilly in the fall sunset. A sharp wind had sprung up, moving the mostly bare limbs of the trees and sending dry leaves skittering here and there over the street, scratching papery sounds on the pavement. The girls stood shivering, neither of them wearing a coat. Cara remembered how hot it had been when she was raking leaves over the weekend; suddenly she wondered if that heat wave had had anything to do with the Burners.

*They carry microclimates with them*, Mrs. Omotoso had said.

Or maybe it was just global warming. Them but not them.

"So what are you going to do with it?" asked Jaye.

When Cara called to ask Jaye to bring the book, her dad had come into the room, so she hadn't been able to explain.

"We're going to try to find Zee," she said now. "And bring her back."

Jaye froze for a second. Then she turned and ran back down to her mother's waiting car. She tapped on the window and then leaned in when her mother rolled it down; after a short discussion, the car was pulling away again.

"Where's she going?" asked Cara when Jaye came back. "What about—don't you have to go to your play practice?"

"She'll pick me up later. I told her we had a big test tomorrow that I'd spaced on. I said you and I needed to cram for it together."

"You're missing rehearsal?"

"You need your friends to make that book work, don't you? So I'm coming."

"Are you sure?" asked Cara. "Last night, because of what I got you into, some man practically *strangled* you. Last night! Are you really OK with going through again?"

"Well, you got hurt, too," said Jaye. "Worse than I did. And you still want to try to help Zee, don't you?"

"But I know her more than you do. And Max is my brother."

Jaye nodded and then spoke slowly.

"It was the worst thing that ever happened to me, that guy having his hands around my neck. For sure. But the rest of it—stepping through that book and being somewhere else—that was the *best* thing that ever happened to me. I mean, the world isn't what I thought it was. Now—life could be anything. The *world* could be anything. It's amazing."

They smiled.


"What does the ward *do*, exactly?" Cara asked Jax when she and Jaye and her two brothers were gathered in her room.

It was dinnertime, but Lolly had turned out to have the evening off, since Cara's dad hadn't expected her or Jax home yet; their dad had his nose buried in papers in his study.

219

He'd said they could forage for lasagna in the fridge.

"Ward lines protect against the old ways—both the Cold's and our own. A ward wouldn't cover guys like Roger, though—unless he was using an old way. It wouldn't do anything to stop a regular person from, say, walking into a regular place and pulling out a regular gun. Far as bad guys like Roger go, it's safe as it ever was. Or wasn't," said Jax.

"So Jax," said Cara, "when Max and Jaye and I go through the windowleaf—if it lets us without Hayley—you stay here. We'll step through the book, and the book will be gone, too. You need to hang tight and stay safe till we get back."

"But before you go," asked Jax, "can you ask the ring where Zee is? Her address? Because I should know it. In case you don't come back. And I have to come after you."

"You *don't* come after us," warned Max. "If we don't come back, you get Dad. You tell him where we went. Tell him what we were trying to do. You hear me?"

Jax nodded stiffly.

"I still need the address," he said.

Cara sat down on her bed, feeling a little self-conscious, since no one had really watched her before except in a crisis situation where she didn't have *time* to feel watched. She closed her eyes, touching the ring with her other hand—which was, she realized, almost completely healed from last night's burns. She asked a question about where—*which town, which road, which house,* was how she phrased it in her head—and thought of Zee.

She saw a sign, WELCOME TO ORLEANS, and then another sign, a light blue one sticking out of an expanse of dried-up grass—BLUEBERRY HOLLOW. Finally she saw the flash of a front door marked fifty-five. It looked like a newer, cookie-cutter-type neighborhood, the kind where all the houses were built at the same time and were the same color.

She opened her eyes again.

"If the ring is right—my vision with the ring—she's near here!" she said, surprised. "In Orleans. A neighborhood called Blueberry Hollow, number fifty-five."

"I can't believe you can do that," said Max. "Really? You just looked up my girlfriend in your head?"

"I could be wrong, Max," she said. "It's mostly the ring."

Max shook his head—half admiring, she thought, and half disbelieving.

"So far so good," said Jax. "Then I can google you. If *that's* allowed by Big Brother."

"Are you ready?" Cara asked Jaye, who'd spread the windowleaf open on the bed.

"Wait!" said Max. "Ask if there's a ward, too. Because from what you told me about last night, we have to land outside it, right?"

"Plus," said Jax, "the ring or the book can't give us data from *across* the ward. That's what the ward's *about*. Protection from objects like this. It's why you could see Mom was at the power plant, but not where she was *inside* it till you stepped past the line. Same here: the book may tell

221

you where Zee is generally, but then you have to cross the ward line to find her."

"So the elementals can't cross them at all?" asked Cara. "Even if it's their side's ward in the first place?"

"Right," said Jax. "Elementals can't cross wards at all, because the wards repel both our works and the enemies, and elementals are purely the Cold One's work. Nonliving. But once you're inside, you should be able to use the ring again."

"So if those elementals can't cross...does that mean once we cross the line, the Burners can't get us?" asked Jaye.

Jax shook his head.

"I wish. But they could be inside *already*. Guarding her. Like they were guarding Mom at the cooling tower."

"Great," said Max.

Before, Cara had leapt before she looked, she thought— and to be impulsive on her own behalf was one thing, but now other people were at stake, too.

"Thanks for that, Jax," she said. "Thank you."

Again she closed her eyes and touched the ring. This time she asked to see the ward line in Blueberry Hollow. And it was hard to see what she was looking at, at first, in the descending dark of twilight. But when she finally made it out, it was surprisingly beautiful: a kind of thin wall of distortion that seemed to rise from the curb up into the air, half reflecting and half absorbing the scenery around it—bushes, houses, telephone wires, and sky. Images stretched and compressed, softened into blurs and then came clear again.

They should land on the street, then step onto the grass. After that they'd find out more.

"OK. So I guess I know where we need to be," she said, opening her eyes.

She and Max and Jaye stood close together beside the bed, where the book was spread open, Max grimacing to cover his embarrassment. Cara repeated the question ritual, and beneath them the pages lost their whiteness as the scene came up: the sign, the curb, the dry grass, and the light blue sides of houses and gray-shingled rooftops. *It was working.* The sky wasn't too visible from this angle, but there was a purple hint of it at the top.

"Holy crap," said Max. The semi-permanent skeptical look was wiped off his face, Cara saw, and felt a surge of pride.

The picture was dizzying to look into, she realized—it was so jarring that this space yawned at their fingertips, this depth and air and world where really, beneath the book, all there should be was a coverlet and sheets and a mattress, and beneath that the floorboards, and so on downwards, in three simple dimensions, through the normal strata of the old house....

"Let's go," she said, and grabbed the hands on each side of her.

They stepped awkwardly up onto the bed, springy beneath their shoes, around the sides of the book with their arms stretching over it. And then they stepped in.

❈

This time it was more of a clamber than a fall, as though they'd stepped down onto the street from a step, like some steps on buses, that was just a bit too high. But they didn't tumble, as they had before.

"Wow!" said Max. "That was rad. That was rad!"

For a moment his eagerness made him sound less like himself and more like Jax.

Cara gave the book to Jaye to hold, looking around at the neighborhood as Max enthused on how amazing it had been to step through the windowleaf. She felt grateful that everything was quiet, and no one was with them on the street; she was glad Max was there. The cookie-cutter houses had some lit windows—though number fifty-five looked pretty dark—but there were no people on the sidewalks, no cars pulling in or out of the driveways.

It was dinnertime here, too, after all.

"She has to have a sleeper, doesn't she? Those are their keepers, sort of," said Jaye, explaining to Max. "You saw her with a little girl, right, Cara? Could that little red-haired girl be it?"

"I doubt a little kid could boss Zee around," said Max.

"If she's a hollow, she's not really Zee, though," said Cara. "You haven't seen them. They're more like robots. Or zombies."

"My point is, though, either way she's probably not alone," said Jaye. "Right?"

"All the ring showed me was the house," said Cara. "I'll ask again when we get past the ward line, if you want...."

224

"Let's just go in," said Max impatiently. "If she's there, I'll find her."

And then they *were* past the line, which, seen with the naked eye instead of through the windowleaf, was so much like nothing at all that she could barely believe it was there. They walked across the grass toward the back of the small cottage, through a waist-high white picket gate. There was the door to the kitchen, a screen and a door with panes of glass; Max reached out quickly and pulled the screen door open.

"Wait!" burst out Jaye. "Assuming she *is* a hollow—I mean, there's no guarantee the Burners won't be watching through her eyes, and then decide to use her! To get to us! You haven't seen them, Max, but the Burners come through the eyes…."

"Cara told me," said Max.

"So how are we going to stop that from happening?"

"We'll just have to just grab her—Max, you'll have to be the one. Grab her and run outside as fast as you can, crossing the ward. Then we'll go back home through the book," said Cara. "And hope we make it through before a Burner can use her."

Max nodded curtly and pushed on the inside door. It wasn't even clicked all the way closed.

"Once we're back, she'll be warded," Cara reminded Jaye. "And then Jax will fix her. OK?"

Jay nodded uncertainly, and Cara smiled to reassure her but felt worried herself. That must be what leadership was: just hoping desperately that you'd turn out to be right.

And then they were in, Max leading.

Inside the lights were off but she could still see the shapes of things around them—the kitchen, long and narrow, with linoleum under their feet; then the hall, with a long, flowery rug. She saw a phone on a table, a kitten calendar on the wall. She grabbed the newel post and swung around onto the stairs, with Jaye right behind her.

"Can't see anyone on the first floor," whispered Max.

None of them wanted to speak out loud in the cottage. It seemed too risky. They made their way softly up the carpeted stairs; at the landing there was a window through which light from streetlamps came through, enough to keep the dark at bay.

"I'm taking the room at the end, you take that one," whispered Max, and went ahead of them down the hall.

Cara and Jaye passed a bathroom with its door ajar; they looked at each other, and then Cara pushed open the next door down.

It was a mostly dark bedroom; a soft light came from a star-shaped nightlight plugged into a wall beside the bed. There was a row of dolls on a shelf, a chest of drawers with flowers on top, a white bed with a sleeping shape nestled under the covers. A tinkly, mechanical little tune was playing from a jewelry box. The box sat propped open on a white chest of drawers, and inside a minuscule plastic ballerina rotated on her small pedestal in jittery motions, wearing a pink tutu, her arms curved over her head.

The bed was straight ahead of them, and someone was asleep in it. But something kept Cara from calling out Zee's name. She stepped toward the bed nervously as Jaye hung back just inside the door to the room. It was so strange to be intruding into someone's *home*...but her mother had said: *Most hollows don't survive the Burners coming through.* She remembered Zee smiling warmly at her on the bus last time they talked, saying *Max said to keep an eye on you.... I'm here if you need anything.* Zee had always been nice to her. Even when Max was blowing her off and treating her as younger and uncool, Zee didn't talk down to her. Zee acted like they were almost the same age.

Then she saw the hair on the head on the pillow: red.

She turned to Jaye and mouthed: *little girl. Not Zee—the little girl.*

Jaye nodded, understanding.

So the little girl had to be captive here, too. Didn't she? She was too little to be anything else; she had to be a victim, either a sleeper or a hollow, and she would be hurt if they left her here, just as Zee would.

Cara stood over the girl. She hesitated.

She could carry the little girl, couldn't she? Carry her through the windowleaf and to safety? Maybe she wouldn't even wake up; maybe she was sleeping like, well, like a baby.... Max was looking for Zee, Max would find her and bring her with him; Cara doubted he'd even let them help. And surely, between them, Cara and Jaye could handle one little girl.

*Let's take her*, she mouthed to Jaye, and at first Jaye didn't get it but then she did, and nodded.

Cara lifted the coverlet carefully—it'd be too hard to bundle her up and lift her with its downy thickness in the way—and she saw the little girl's flannel nightgown stretching over her back; she was facing away from Cara, a worn stuffed animal peeking over her shoulder. A teddy bear? She leaned down and slid her arms under the girl, warm and snoring lightly. And then she lifted.

She was far heavier than Cara had expected, and then, oh no! She was waking up!

She turned in Cara's arms, dropping her bear—it wasn't a bear, Cara recognized in the background of her mind; it had long teeth—and then her face was there. Right up close to Cara's.

And she wasn't a little girl.

Wasn't a girl at all.

Cara dropped her instantly, stifling a scream. Behind her, Jaye was screaming for Max. Down on the bed the little not-girl sat up, smiling. The smile was hungry, the eyes were huge—black and huge!—and the little girl was actually an old lady, her hair a fake, dyed red, with fat apple-doll cheeks and smeared lipstick and blue eyeshadow and rotting teeth. Her breath was terrible.

She was a tiny old lady, a lady with enormous, hollowing eyes who was clearly…even without those eyes, she wasn't OK. She wasn't normal. She was something Cara had never seen, like a child aged prematurely. There was a viciousness to her face. She was ghoulish.

And behind the bed, on the shelf on the wall, the row of dolls stared down at them, and the dolls were old too, Cara registered with a part of her that was distant from the old woman—old, old and dusty, with frozen porcelain grins. Suddenly the whole room felt different: the tinkly song from the jewelry box was eerie; the flowers on the bedside table were long dead and crawling with bugs.

"Cara!" yelled Jaye, behind her. "Come *on!*"

For the old lady was rising from the bed. As Cara stepped back—she couldn't help screaming—the old lady reached out for her. She was grasping and scrabbling at Cara's arms her long and yellow fingernails. Her toenails were long and yellow, too, on the bare feet on the carpet, and she was grinning and scrabbling at Cara's wrists, trying to get ahold of them. She grabbed at Cara's left hand, and as she did so her big eyes were even bigger, expanding in her face, and Cara staggered backwards, trying desperately to pull away.

"The Burners! The Burners are coming!" shouted Jaye, terrified by the old woman's eyes.

The old lady was pulling so hard at Cara's wrist that Cara was afraid the skin might tear; her nails were digging into Cara's fingers, but Cara pulled free and staggered back, and she and Jaye were out the bedroom door, and Max was there, too, half colliding with them, his face an inquiry into how scared he should be, and he caught Jaye's eyes and decided to panic too, and then all three of them were pounding down the stairs, fumbling with the lock on the front door and racing through the yard. They leapt off the curb, past the wardline, and into the street. Jaye dropped the book and Max pulled it open.

But then Cara felt something behind her, grasping hands, and there was the woman, dreadful with her smeared makeup and ragged hair, dreadful with her ferocious grin and the spreading black eyes that were eating up her face, and she had Cara's left hand again.

Cara turned away and focused—the book was her only saving grace, she knew—and squeezed her own eyes shut and thought of home, her bedroom and her home, thought hard while Jaye and Max were grabbing her other hand and arm. She thought of where they had to go and reached her right hand back to touch the ring on her left, her fingers at the same time touching the old lady's, too, which were bony and hard, and it was all a rotten, horrified wrestle. A long, ragged pain shot through Cara's left-hand fingers, and the old lady screeched, a high, terrible screech.

They were stepping forward, Cara and Jaye and Max, just as the smell of burning came to Cara, the smell of singed hair in her nostrils, and they knocked heads and shoulders into each other as they fell, and her finger tore.

❦

She'd never loved her own bed as much as she did landing there: a trusted place. Even the slightly dirty but familiar smell of her sheets—which told her right away where she was as she hit them—was comforting.

Still, for a moment she rubbernecked, confused, and scrambling to right herself, half sure the terrible woman was close on their heels. Max and Jaye were practically on top of her, like in a game of Twister; they all got off the bed and stood there, breathing hard.

The windowleaf had fallen beside them on a pillow, and Jax was sitting a few feet away. He looked up startled from his laptop.

"You're bleeding!" he said.

She raised her left hand slowly, stunned, and saw a slice down the length of one finger, blood running down her arm. It stung. She felt it strongly as soon as she saw it—as though the pain had receded when she wasn't paying attention to it but, once seen, came back again.

"She scratch—scratched me—" she started limply, and then she knew *why* the woman had scratched her.

Because her bloody finger was bare. The ring was gone.

"My nazar!"

"What *was* that?" asked Jaye, pale and still panting a little. "What was *she*?"

"Did you find Zee?" asked Jax.

"She was sleeping," said Max breathlessly. "Literally sleeping. This deep, deep sleep. I couldn't wake her. I was going to pick her up. But then I heard you guys screaming about the Burners…. Can I go back? I need to get her. *I've got to go back!*"

"Are you *kidding*?" asked Jaye, incredulous.

"The old lady's a hollow. They were just about to come through. Didn't you smell the burning as we stepped? If you went now, she'd be waiting for you—you'd get burned, Max!" said Cara. She swallowed with a painfully parched throat and then saw an old, stale glass of water on her nightstand; she reached out and gulped it down.

"What old lady?" asked Jax, looking from her to Max and back again.

She didn't want to explain, so she just nodded at him, with the nod that had come to mean he could ping. It only took a second for him to know everything.

"So it was—was it a trap?" asked Jaye.

"Zee's not a hollow, is she?" asked Max. "I mean, her eyes were closed. But she looked normal. "

"It sounds to me like she's a sleeper," said Jax to Max, and then to Cara, "And the old lady took your ring? We need to figure out if it was planned in advance."

Jaye walked across to the bathroom that joined Cara's room to Jax's. She ran water into the sink and splashed it on her face, then opened the medicine cabinet, pulled out a box of Band-Aids, and came back over to them.

"Zee's a sleeper?" echoed Max.

"Here," said Jaye, peeling off a wrapper and holding the strip over Cara's bleeding finger. "No, this won't work. It's a really long cut. I think we need one of the bigger ones…."

Her hands were shaking, Cara saw, as she rummaged around in the box for a larger bandage. They were all still having aftershocks.

"I hope she didn't—I mean, I hope there isn't anything *in* the cut," said Jax. "Like with that pen…"

"Her nails were disgusting," said Jaye with a shudder as she tilted Cara's hand to put on the bigger bandage.

"So either this—this hollow was *supposed* to entice you, and then take your ring, or somehow when you showed up she just recognized its value and grabbed for it," said Jax. "Hard to know which. I *hope* it wasn't planned, because if it was, they're spying on us—really closely. And then—also Zee might have been a part of it. I mean, luring us there."

"Bull," said Max. "I saw her sleeping there. She's a victim!"

"I guess the ring was still on my finger long enough to get us back through the book," mused Cara, looking down at the cut. "But now we've lost them both. Both of the old-ways objects. Because I can't *use* the windowleaf anymore. Not without the ring."

"So even if we could get close to Zee, we couldn't do it with these—these tricks of yours," said Max. "We'd have to get to Orleans like everyone else does. Driving."

Because of her, Zee was still stranded, still in danger, and on top of that their tools were gone, the miraculous equipment. It was her fault for leading them into this, hoping she was doing the right thing…. Well, she hadn't been right. She'd been wrong. They should have consulted someone else about Zee—someone who had a few years on them.

What if they could never get to Zee now?

"The little girl—I mean the not-little girl—you know. She was a dwarf, I think," said Jaye. "A hollow who was also a dwarf. We have a little person in my family, married to my aunt. I think that lady was one, too."

"So say I drive over there," interrupted Max, who seemed to be in his own distracted world and barely listening to what the others said. "You're saying I'll be screwed, right? You're saying some Burning Man's going to come out through her eyes the second I get near?"

"Not her eyes," said Jax. "At least, I don't think so. The old lady is the hollow in that pair, and I think the sleeper is Zee. That means she may not even *know* what she is. She may show up at school tomorrow acting like nothing's any different from usual. But the thing is, she's under their control. Whenever they want her to be. And, yeah, the hollow is a major obstacle. Cara said there was already a Burner coming when you took off."

Max stared at him, then pressed his lips together and looked out the window, shaking his head.

"I'm gonna go call her dad," he said after a minute. "Even if it's dangerous, I can't just leave her. No way. I have to tell him where she is."

And he walked out of the room.

"You know what the scariest part is, in a way?" said Jaye into the silence that followed. "I mean, once she *was* a little girl with red hair. And now…she's that."

Then her cell rang; her mother was out front, waiting to take her home.

"Gotta go," she said.

She stood up and looked down at Cara's arm, patterned with a line of drying blood whose drips branched off it like a tree.

"Jaye," said Cara, and stretched out her other hand to take her friend's. "Thanks for trusting me enough to come along. Thank you for trying to help Zee."

"Hey," said Jaye. "It makes my skin crawl to think of that lady's fingernails. But I'm glad we did it, too."

⚜

After Jaye went home, Cara had a shower, slipped into her ratty but clean old pajamas, neatly laundered and folded into her top drawer by Lolly, and curled up in her bed with a book. A little after nine, Jax padded through her door in his sockfeet—he had a way of wearing his socks so the sock toes hung emptily off the ends of his own toes and flopped around looking absurd.

"Max says Zee's dad drove right over to that place and brought her home," he reported. "And nothing happened to him. He didn't even *see* the old lady. Zee woke up and couldn't remember how she got there. It sounded like she got in a lot of trouble. Her dad's pissed. He thinks she was underage drinking or something."

Still, it was a relief: Zee was safe, and back in her normal life again.

Unless she was just pretending.

And now they'd have to be at school with her. At *home* with her. Not knowing what she might be.

"Great. So now we're stuck with Max's girlfriend. Who just may be a lethal weapon."

235

"At least she's not a hollow. I'm pretty sure of that. And if she *is* a sleeper—instead of just having been some kind of hostage or victim, like Mom was—then we'll know who her hollow is, right? We'll recognize her right away. Or at least you and Jaye and Max will. Zee might be a spy, but she can't burn anyone. No Burner can come through *her*."

"So we're supposed to act normal with a spy for the Cold One in our midst?"

"Maybe Max will stop hanging out with her," said Jax.

Cara locked eyes with him.

"Like, break up?"

She thought about it for a second but came to a dead end. She could only think how much she liked Zee—how nice she'd always been.

They were interrupted by a knock on the bedroom door, which had to be their dad, since Max hardly ever knocked.

"Come in!" said Cara.

"Open it for me, please," came their dad's voice. "No hands free."

Jax jumped up and went over; their dad had a steaming mug in each hand.

"Made you some hot chocolate," he said. "And then it's bedtime, right?"

"Cool," said Jax, taking a mug. "Thanks, Dad."

"So, homework all done, Cara?"

"There wasn't any," she said as he handed her the other mug and sat down beside Jax on her bed. "Because we were away at the meet."

236

With their mother gone, their dad seemed to think he had two basic jobs as a parent: one, provide food; two, mention homework. That was his daily checklist, more or less, when he emerged from the cave of his study. When her mother was here, he hadn't even had those jobs, really. All he'd had to worry about then was doing his teaching and writing, making the family pancakes for breakfast once a week, and now and then jiggling the flusher on a toilet that wouldn't stop running.

"Don't worry about us, Dad," she said on impulse. "We're fine. I'm really sorry about going AWOL in Boston. You know I don't usually act like that. I was just worried about Jax. And you know Mrs. M, she can be kind of…you know, overprotective."

"It may seem like that to you," said her dad, the corners of his eyes crinkling with a smile that was part affection and part reproach. "But she has her reasons."

He leaned forward and kissed Jax on the top of the head, then stood up and leaned over Cara to do the same. "Back to your own room, Jax. And tomorrow, over dinner, I expect a full report on your time at the Institute. OK?"

When Jax and her dad had gone to their bedrooms—or at least Jax to his bedroom and their father to his study—a comfortable silence rose around her. The house felt pleasantly familiar, like it was settling down for the night in the same way that it always had. But she knew the silence might change its tone while she lay there, if she let the image of the old woman prey on her as she tried to get to sleep. It might become more threatening.

The homey, chirping crickets of the summer were gone now; there was only the wind rattling the loose wooden shutters on the outside of the house. If she held her breath, she could hear the faint sound of it sweeping through the trees that were holding onto their dying leaves.

And it might not be so easy to block out what had happened, because the long cut on her finger, beneath the Band-Aid, still stung dully. The cut from that sharp, curved, dirty fingernail—

She shivered. She might keep a light on. Just a small one. Just for tonight. Sure it was childish, but anyone might want to who'd been clawed by that—that person who wasn't a child but a fake child, a trick. Who seemed like a demon.

Not a night light, though. Maybe her desk lamp.

Something caught her eye on a high shelf in the corner of her room. It was an old music box printed with a design of flowers and leaves that her mother had given her. It didn't have a ballerina inside, but it did have a fairy, she recalled— a slender fairy with plastic wings, which turned and turned to tinkling music like the dancer in the old woman's room.

She got out of bed and reached up for it, then tucked it away in her closet, covered with a favorite sweater, and closed the closet door. She felt a pang, because it had come from her mother, but she couldn't bear to look at it now.

Then she turned off the overhead, flicked on the desk lamp, and got into bed.

But she still had one thing left to do.

She slipped her cell out of her backpack on the desk beside her and speed-dialed Hayley. She was betting her friend wouldn't pick up; she wanted to leave a message anyway. She'd feel better, trying to fall asleep, if she could at least do that.

It rang three times, and then, just before it seemed it would go to voice mail, she heard Hayley's voice.

"Hey."

"Oh!" said Cara. "I didn't think you'd pick up. I know you're upset with me."

There was a pause.

"I'm sorry that I dragged you back into all of this," she went on. "I know you wanted to stay and have fun; that was the whole reason you were excited about going to the meet in the first place. I *know* you only do the swim-team thing in the first place to hang with people. It was just, when I asked you guys to come to the Institute I was really afraid for Jax—you saw how he was—and I felt alone, and…I looked at this painting, at the Institute, and your face was there, along with Jaye's. I needed you guys. I couldn't have brought my mom to him without you. And I mean, you were amazing. Knowing what cooling towers were…. You didn't even complain that your eyebrows got singed half off. Plus, your confidence really helped Jaye, I think. So I'm really grateful, and I'm sorry. And I want to let you know that—you don't have to be a part of the craziness anymore. *Whatever* it is. You can have a regular fun life. Just because you're my best friend doesn't mean you have to—you know, be involved with everything I'm involved with. Especially when it's so weird. And so terrifying."

There was quiet on the other end of the line again after Cara's long speech. Which was downright unnatural for Hayley. Cara almost kept talking, to fill up space and cover the tension, but then decided she should wait. It was Hayley's turn.

"And *I* know you only do dance committee and all that noise to keep me company," said Hayley finally, her voice sounding weak. "I do. So I'm sorry also. I'm sorry I acted like this. It was actually pretty lame."

Cara let her breath out.

"Because," said Hayley, "you tease me about being superficial and like that. But my mom talks about character. And how it's fine to care about fashion and all that, as long as you have *character* beneath, real character that knows right from wrong. And not only knows it but is willing to fight for it. Even if it's not convenient. Otherwise you're, like, soulless. And it seemed like Jaye was really fighting for it, for you and your family, and I got afraid…that, you know, you were starting to like her more than me."

"Hayley! No way. It's not true!"

"So I'm the one who's sorry. And I don't want to be left out. I do want to help. Even if it, well. Messes with my schedule."

"Hay," said Cara gently after some seconds passed. "Thank you for that. It means a lot to me."

"But FYI? I *am* totally pissed about the eyebrows," said Hayley.

They laughed, relieved.

"I'm going to have to pencil them in till they grow back," she said. "And let's face it, the pencil-brow look is over. That look is way creepy."

Cara told her about the terrible old woman, about Zee.

"I told you she was evil, didn't I?"

"It's not *her*, Hayley," rebuked Cara, but she was grinning ruefully: even in her wisest moments, Hayley was still jealous.

Then they talked about small, normal things for a short time until they both felt tired and hung up. Laying her cheek against her pillow, she felt satisfied knowing Hayley and Jaye were still with her. They were with her even though she *hadn't* gotten everything right, even though sometimes her being wrong had ended up hurting them.

But they were still with her. They trusted that she was trying her best.

She thought of the flying reptile, Q, so bizarre—both beautiful and not beautiful. She thought of the catfish and the otter that had been her mother, and how there, at least, her instincts had been right, even though she denied them because it seemed downright impossible. She thought of Jax, looking for ants on his windowsill—the tiny ants that it turned out might be against them. She hoped not; other than when they bit her, she'd always admired ants, how they could carry things so many times more massive than their whole bodies.

241

She thought of the giant squid and other glowing animals in the deep abyss, fleeing in terror, swept forward by that hulking vehicle with its dim red light; she felt terrible for them, for how they'd been mowed under by that vast and dark machine.

She *did* want to keep helping her mother, she thought. No: she needed to. Despite the Pouring Man, the sleepers and the Burners, despite people like Roger, who'd looked right at her and smiled and handed her poison. She wanted to help her mother keep the world safe, not only for herself and the people she knew but for all these other mysterious beings who were sharing it with them. She didn't even *know* all of them, not by a long shot—there was a universe of creatures out there she still had to discover.

*I'll go to sleep*, she thought. *I'll go to sleep and dream of everything there could be.*

*Lydia Millet (lydiamillet.net) is the author of many novels for* adult readers, including *My Happy Life*, which won the PEN-USA Award for Fiction in 2003, *Oh Pure and Radiant Heart*, about the scientists who designed the first atomic bomb, which was shortlisted for the UK's Arthur C. Clarke Prize, and *Ghost Lights*. Her story collection *Love in Infant Monkeys* was a finalist for the 2010 Pulitzer Prize. She has taught at Columbia University and the University of Arizona and now works as a writer and editor at an endangered-species protection group. *The Shimmers in the Night* is her second novel for young readers following *The Fires Beneath the Sea*.

She is working on the third book in the Dissenters series.

**DATE DUE**